Cool for America

Cool for America

Stories

Andrew Martin

Farrar, Straus and Giroux | New York

Farrar, Straus and Giroux
120 Broadway, New York 10271

Several of these stories previously appeared, in slightly different
form, in the following publications: *The Paris Review* ("Cool for
America," "With the Christopher Kids," "No Cops," "Childhood,
Boyhood, Youth"), *ZYZZYVA* ("A Dog Named Jesus," as
"The Wedding Stray"), *The Los Angeles Review of Books Quarterly*
("The Changed Party"), *The Atlantic* ("Deep Cut"), and
The Yale Review ("Short Swoop, Long Line").

Library of Congress Control Number: 2020931132
ISBN: 978-0-374-10816-8

Designed by Gretchen Achilles

Our books may be purchased in bulk for promotional,
educational, or business use. Please contact your local bookseller
or the Macmillan Corporate and Premium Sales Department at
1-800-221-7945, extension 5442, or by e-mail at
MacmillanSpecialMarkets@macmillan.com.

www.fsgbooks.com
www.twitter.com/fsgbooks • www.facebook.com/fsgbooks

1 3 5 7 9 10 8 6 4 2

For my sisters, Sara and Caroline,
and in memory of Greta Yegyan

Contents

Cool for America

No Cops

THE ANTS HAD GOTTEN IN through the shattered bottom half of Leslie's laptop screen. Now they crawled across her green-and-blue-tinted Word documents and websites one or two at a time, with no discernible pattern or destination. It must have been a hell of a place for an ant, all that glowing landscape to be negotiated, possibly forever. It wasn't clear whether any ants ever escaped or if they all just died in there. If they were dying, they at least had the decency to do it over in the dark border area of the screen or down in the keyboard, rather than within her line of sight. She was trying to see how long she could go without buying a new computer. The sound of crackling glass every time she opened the screen suggested that the reckoning was nigh.

She was on her front porch, trying to make herself write an email to her ex-boyfriend Marcus, who was, she had just learned, due back in town in a week for an exhibition of his drawings at a local gallery. (Well, *exhibition*, *gallery*—his work was being featured in the basement of the camera store in downtown Missoula.) She wanted to tell him that he shouldn't be worried about running into her, that she no longer had any loose feelings about the breakup, that she thought it would be nice to have a drink, even, if he found himself with some time on his hands. But these thoughts wouldn't form themselves into coherent sentences on the screen, maybe because she wasn't sure they were true. She hadn't forgotten the ugly melodrama of their final months together and she hadn't forgiven him for going off to Italy for a fellowship without her, like a punk-ass. The worst thing about studying art history was the artists.

Her newish man, a mannish boy, was named Cal, for the baseball player, he claimed, though Cal Ripken would have only been a rookie when he was born, so it was probably made up, like Hillary being named after the Everest climber. Anyway, he *was* from Baltimore originally. Like many of the men she knew in Missoula, he was a dog trainer, novelist, and organic grocery store employee. His sweaters had moth holes in them. He rolled his own cigarettes. His novels weren't self-published, technically, but only because one of his friends in town printed and distributed the books for him. His friend's service fee was mostly offset by the handful of sales Cal made at his readings, which were attended with shrugging obligation by his friends and the town's mostly elderly patrons of the arts. There was, in fact, a reading that night at Marlowe's Books for his latest opus, a four-hundred-page novel set in Butte on New Year's Eve, 1899.

It wasn't ideal to date a bad—or, okay, flagrantly

mediocre—writer, but it wasn't as terrible as she'd worried it might be. Cal had decent, if very male, taste in books (Bolaño, Roth, David Foster Wallace) and wasn't aggressively dumb about most things. He also, blessedly, lacked ambition; he didn't seem too stressed out during the composition of his books, and he didn't seem to worry about the fact that no one outside of Montana, and few people within it, would ever read them. He was smart enough not to push it, and that counted for something. And, frankly, she wasn't in a great position to judge his work or his choices, given her own life situation (this being a polite euphemism for depressed and barely employed), but she did know what was good and what wasn't. This hadn't blossomed into an ethical dilemma yet. Politeness and desire and taste did not all have to be mutually exclusive, did they? And maybe it was his lack of anxiety about his literary status that made him so good in bed. Leave it to somebody else to pierce the human heart with punctuation.

She gave up on her email to Marcus for now. She picked up the laptop—one hand supporting the bottom, the other cradling the fragile spine—and went back into her apartment through the propped-open front door. She laid the computer on the couch gingerly and got a beer from the refrigerator, then drank it in the kitchen, staring out the window at the parking lot, thinking about Marcus.

She was five minutes late for her copyediting gig at the *Open Door*, and Lyle called her out for smelling like booze. But what was the point of working for an *alternative* paper if you were supposed to show up sober? She was told to start with the fourteen-page "community calendar" as punishment. "Join BodyWorks from 3:00–4:00 p.m. for a free workshop on mindful living and stress reduction. Kids and pets welcome!" Sounded reasonable. There was a bluegrass band at one brewery, "crafts for charity" at another, and a scandalously cheap happy hour at the new distillery. Kids and pets were welcome. A rap-metal band last heard from in 1998 was playing the Wilma. And yes, on Friday, "Drawings from Life" by Marcus Cull was being displayed in the basement of the Compound Eye as part of First Friday, 5:00–7:00 p.m. She considered using her copyediting powers for evil—dogs and firstborns executed on sight?—but Lyle had a tendency to check her work, especially when she'd been drinking. She changed her ex's name to "Markass Krill," hoping this might be subtle enough to slip through the censor's net.

She got a text from Cal—"Gonna read chapter 8 good choice yes/no?" Was chapter eight the mine cave-in? The dissolution of the affair between the former slave and the alcoholic homesteader? Cal's books tended to be quite—one might even say gratuitously—violent, and she hoped he wouldn't read one of the many sequences of mangling or disfigurement. He'd gotten the idea, from movies and Cormac McCarthy, presumably, that the best way to depict "the past" was through unrepentant brutality, because that's how it *was*. Maybe, she thought, better not to depict it at all, then. She responded to his text with an equivocal "yeh?"

It was hard, sometimes, putting up with the town's

cheerful, half-assed shtick, but most days the alterna-
tives seemed worse. New York was a nightmare of pointless
ambition, people waiting in endless lines for nothing. In
Boston they didn't bother with lines—they just jammed as
many white people as possible into anyplace showing the
Pats. She'd spent her early years in Princeton, with its liberal
old-money complacency, dominated by "good families"
who produced "good kids," most of them zapped awful by
divorce and private school. They'd never get her back there
alive, at least not for more than a long weekend. She'd spent
her childhood wanting to be from somewhere else, anywhere that didn't draw a wince. Of course, name recognition was the whole appeal for her mother—when people
asked where she lived, she could just say, "Princeton," and
they'd know she was a person of wealth and taste, whereas
when people asked Leslie, she said, "Jersey," then, if pressed,
"Hopewell Valley, in Mercer County? Near Princeton?"
Which was true—one good thing about New Jersey was
that there were so many townships and villages and what
have you that you could always just claim the nearest one
that appealed. In Montana, the categories were broader. You
were from Back East, Around Here, or California. It was
best to not be from California.

She moved on to copyediting the arts section, her favorite part of the job. She hoped that if she hung around
the office making snappy comments for long enough, she
might someday be allowed to write a film or concert review.
The current movie critic, Amy Freitch, trashed almost
everything she saw in a biting, faux-naïve voice, saving
her praise, it seemed, only for films about martial arts and

animals. Leslie had gone camping with her once, and they'd taken mushrooms and read tarot cards. Amy claimed to know how to do it, but seemed to be making things up as she went along, possibly because she was hallucinating too much to interpret what the cards portended, probably just because she thought it was funny. Nevertheless, she'd predicted a hard year for Leslie, which had proved accurate. But wasn't every year a hard year? Even a *good* year took a lot out of you.

Amy was sexy in a way that Leslie envied—boyish in her carelessness about clothes and posture but still long-haired and vulnerable. She also drank too much, like most of the people Leslie admired. She hoped that Amy would get a job writing for a real newspaper so that Leslie could take her place at the *Door*. She wouldn't be as good as Amy right away, but she'd find her voice. "A voice like a girl with ants in her laptop," they'd say, "marching in dissolved and scattered ranks toward some obscure but essential truth." Most people she talked to disliked Amy's pieces, so maybe she'd get fired. Leslie couldn't in good conscience hope for that, but, well, it was out of her hands, wasn't it?

Amy's piece was pretty clean, but the week's book review, of an eco-memoir about the grasslands of Eastern Montana, was a mess. It was by a recent graduate of the MFA program, an eco-poet who couldn't, or chose not to, organize his sentences in the traditional manner. Nature careth not about such frivolities, but even an alternative weekly required the occasional comma. She spent a solid hour rewriting the piece, knowing she'd catch shit for being overzealous. But she didn't want to contribute to the prevailing idea that everyone born after 1984 operated in a vacuum of good intentions without recourse to actual knowledge.

Despite her rejection of its trappings, Leslie had been thoroughly and expensively educated, and some of the content had stuck, even as she'd worked hard to smother her recollection of it under a scratchy blanket of booze and "other." Oh, she was an expert on "encountering the other," and she wasn't talking about UM's shit show of a diversity fair. She missed cocaine, but there wasn't much of it in town, and the couple of times she *had* run across it, it was awful. The grungy kids did heroin—it was back! again!— but she'd always been afraid of that. She wanted to kill time but not, you know, *kill* it. Like, permanently.

She arrived at the bookstore a half hour before Cal's reading so she could look at books and help set up. There was a local itinerant man sprawled on the sidewalk next to the door. He was moaning and slowly kicking his legs like he was swimming.

"Are you all right?" Leslie said loudly.

The man moaned louder and kicked with more purpose, in her direction. She went into the bookstore. Kim was behind the desk staring intently at the store's computer screen.

"Have you seen that guy out front?" Leslie said.

"I don't want to call the cops on him," Kim said, eyes

still on the screen. "But if Max gets here and he's still out there, he's not going to be happy. Mostly I don't want to deal with it."

"He doesn't seem to be in a position to be reasoned with."

"Accurate."

Leslie wandered among the new-books tables, browsing through the poetry and the stuff from the independent presses. How the store stayed in business selling such strange and unpopular books remained its enduring mystery. There must have been enough people buying them to sustain the small shop, but Leslie never seemed to meet them. Secret intellectuals, speak up! Reveal yourselves!

The big problem that Leslie had, as far as she could tell, was that she was still, at twenty-seven, a person without well-established and verifiable thoughts or opinions about things. Other people were moving through the world and analyzing what they saw with some kind of consistency, a set of values that was sustainable and based on . . . something. What they grew up with, what they had developed later in opposition to what their parents had told them. Of course, she knew that there was no such thing as a *balanced consciousness*, or, if there was, it existed primarily in idiots and self-satisfied creeps, men mostly, who chose not to question their lives for fear of realizing they were terrible failures. But still. Everyone else always seemed to be doing better at it than she was.

"You want to help me with the chairs and stuff?" Kim said, finally turning to her.

"Sure."

Kim was one of the good ones, a seriously noncomplacent person. She struggled openly with the borders of her life. She was writing a memoir about her peripatetic childhood, much of which involved traveling the country in a van with her family, moving between cultish New Age communities in dire poverty. Kim's rejection of her family was partial and unhappy. She loved them and forgave them in principle but also had to stay away from them and have almost no contact with them whatsoever because most of their interactions triggered major depressive episodes.

Leslie had been at the Rose with Kim one night when Kim got a call from an unknown number. Usually she screened such calls, but she was drunk and expecting to hear from a man she'd recently slept with, so she answered it. Leslie watched as Kim listened in silence for a minute to someone speaking on the other end, and then held down the power button until the phone turned off.

"So that was my father?" she said. "I'm going to need you to hang with me for the rest of the night. Sorry."

Then they'd gotten ugly drunk—drink-spilling, falling-off-of-barstools, shouting-at-the-TV drunk. Jamie had been there, blessedly, to drive them home, and they'd lain on the hardwood floor of Kim's apartment, curled up against each other, Kim's hair in Leslie's face.

"I really hope I don't puke in your hair," Leslie said.

"If there's any chance of that, you should not stay there," Kim said.

"I'm sorry your family's so fucked up," Leslie said.

"It's okay. I deserve it."

"You were bad in a past life."

"Past, present, future. There is no temporal zone in which I have not been, or will not be, a terrible person."

"What did you ever do to anybody?"

"Nothing," Kim said. "Not appreciated the gifts God gave me."

"Well, what are you supposed to do?"

"Help people. Do something besides be selfish and wasteful."

"You will," Leslie said. "We're still just little babies."

"Drunk-ass babies," Kim said. "Look out, America: the babies found the liquor cabinet."

"This week's episode: Babies get their stomachs pumped. Bad, bad babies."

And more like that. They'd both thrown up eventually, Leslie in the middle of the night, Kim in the morning, though they'd made it to a trash can and the toilet, respectively. Respectably.

"Do you know this other girl who's reading tonight?" Kim said.

"I didn't know there *was* anybody else," Leslie said.

"Megan D'Onofrio?" Kim said. "Lyric essayist?"

"Weren't essays bad enough before they got lyrical?"

"Maybe she's cool. Let's try really, really hard to be open-minded. That might be interesting."

"Do you have weed?" Leslie said.

"Yes!"

"My mind is open to smoking your weed."

They went out to the alley behind the store, Kim carrying a box full of unsold literary magazines with the front covers ripped off for recycling. Leslie stood in the spot closer to the street as a lookout while Kim leaned against the wall and loaded the one-hitter painted to look like a cigarette. Their furtiveness was mostly for fun—they were aware of exactly no one who'd had any trouble getting stoned in Missoula. Still, Leslie found it hard to strike the surreptitious East Coast habits she'd developed as a teen during the late, feeble years of the war on drugs, even as, she'd been told, you could now smoke a joint on the street in Manhattan without fear of anything more than a ticket, at least if you were white.

"Yo, hit this," Kim said, and Leslie did.

"We sold, like, three books today," Kim said. "And they were, like, the gluten-free cookbook. All of them."

Leslie passed the piece back.

"Is Max, what, selling organs on the side?" Leslie said.

"I wish he'd cut me in if he was," said Kim, exhaling smoke. "I think he might just be rich somehow."

Leslie took another hit.

"How's the book coming?" she said.

"What are you, my agent?" Kim said.

"Sorry for being curious about your stupid life ambitions," Leslie said.

"It's going slow, man." She looked down the barrel of the one-hitter and then tapped the ash out against the wall. "You think, like, *Oh, it's my life, I can write that, I went to graduate school.* But you have to not hate what you write, you know? Which is hard if you hate yourself to begin with."

"Maybe you should try not writing about yourself," Leslie said.

"Who'd want to read *that*?" Kim said.

They went back into the bookstore, which was dim following the late-afternoon glare. Leslie was surprised by the sharp vertigo of despair—stoned in the company of her favorite friend, surrounded by good books. She had to admit that she was dreading Cal's arrival and subsequent reading. She knew this was unkind, but lying to herself wasn't going very well. Her attempt at self-deception involved rehearsing dramatic internal monologues of uncertainty. *Well, I don't know I'm unhappy. Thinking that Cal depresses me doesn't mean he* actually *depresses me.* But she knew, underneath these contortions, that if one had these thoughts for long enough, self-obfuscated or otherwise, one would eventually need to act on them.

"You okay?" Kim said.

Leslie looked up and realized she'd been standing at the poetry table unconsciously holding a waifish new Anne Carson hardcover.

"Can I use the computer for a minute?" she said.

"Let me just close out for the day," Kim said. "Unless you're buying that."

"Right, like I'm going to just *buy a book*," Leslie said. "Oh, look at me, I'm contributing to the local economy by purchasing important literature."

"It does sound pretty dumb when you say it in that voice. Computer's yours."

Leslie fell into the padded swivel chair and opened her email. It seemed important to write this on a computer instead of her phone. In two blurry minutes—the pot helped, if that was really the right verb—she typed out a truncated version of the gracious, medium-true email to Marcus she'd been drafting in her head for days. She hoped all was well, was glad he was coming to town, hoped they could interact without issue. She signed it "With love, Les," deleted that, retyped it, deleted it again, retyped it again, and hit send. Then she hurriedly logged out of her email, closed the Internet browser, and shut down the computer.

"Whoosh!" she yelled, and held her arms outstretched.

"Um," Kim said. "Does that mean you're ready to help me move the tables?"

They were unfolding the last of the chairs when Cal arrived with the beer, thirty-six jumbo cans from the brewery down the street, purchased at a bulk discount because they'd been badly dented during the production process.

"That guy out front's in rough shape," Cal said. "I tried to talk to him but he wasn't having it."

"You could call the police," Kim said.

"That's fucked up," Cal said.

"Right, well, that's as far as we got, too."

"Nervous?" Leslie said.

"What, me worry?" Cal said. "I have faith in my material."

Kim rolled her eyes behind his back.

Over the next fifteen minutes, the usual suspects wandered into the store, stepping around the drunken man. Max, the owner, was one of the last to arrive.

"How long has that guy been out there?" he said to Kim.

"Oh, him?" Kim said. "I guess he just showed up."

"Come *on*, Kimberly," Max said. He sat down behind the desk and put his head in his hands.

"Leslie, come help me," Kim said. She hooked Leslie's arm through hers and went outside. The man was sprawled to the left of the door, his head resting on his outstretched arm, which extended into the entranceway.

"*Sir*," Kim yelled. "I'm really *sorry* but you *need* to *move* now, *okay*?"

He grunted and shifted slightly, revealing a puddle of urine.

"*Sir*, we don't want to call the police, but you *have* to move *now*."

"No cops," he muttered. He opened his eyes and fixed them unfocusedly on Leslie. She told herself that she understood this, sympathized with it. She knew what it was like to have done too much, to be out of control. She also knew, or suspected, at least, that this really wasn't like that, and that whatever sympathy she had for him was just pity, which she was trying to keep ahead of disgust in her emotional calculus.

"No cops," the man said again, and began dragging himself down the sidewalk, leaving a trail of piss and garbage in his wake. They watched as he re-settled a few storefronts down, curling himself up in the doorway of the closed secondhand clothing store.

"Maybe we *should* call the cops?" Leslie said. "I mean, *fuck*, jail is better than *that*."

"No, it's not," Kim said.

They went back into the store, where a few people had

begun drifting in and picking up cans of Cal's deformed beer.

"Hey, Les, this is Megan," Cal said. "She's my opening act. Or rather, I'm the, uh, cool-down mix to her energizing jams."

Megan acknowledged this with a stifled laugh and shook Leslie's hand. Megan was unusually tall and long-limbed and delicate. Leslie thought Megan was raising her eyebrows ironically but it turned out that was just how they were all the time.

"I'm looking forward to hearing your stuff," Leslie said.

Megan shrugged.

"*I* think it's good, at least," she said.

"That's a start," said Leslie. "What are you reading?"

"It's kind of a reflection on . . . I don't know." She let out a heavy sigh. "The body? I don't really know what I'm doing anymore. It's just . . . it's really *hard*, you know?" She stared down at the floor.

"I'm sure you're going to be great," Leslie said. "This is a very forgiving audience."

"Oh *God*," she said, "I hope I don't have to be *forgiven* for anything."

Once the reading was under way, Leslie found it impossible to stay focused on what Megan was saying. The essay was as amorphous as advertised. It seemed to be about her body, and . . . icebergs? And her father, who was . . . also an iceberg? Leslie checked her phone and was disconcerted to see that she already had a response from Marcus. She had imagined—*hoped* was too strong a word—that he wouldn't reply at all, that her email would simply be registered in her karmic ledger without any need for it to be acknowledged in actual reality. But here was Marcus, alive in her in-box. She looked up and saw that she was attracting a glare from her seatmate, an older woman with a long braid of white hair whom she'd seen at past readings. The woman pointed at Leslie, then at the reader at the lectern. Leslie pointed at her phone.

"I'm texting!" she said in a stage whisper. *"Sorry, I'm too busy texting!"*

This drew smirks from her friends sitting in the row in front of them, but she did put her phone in her bag. She wasn't as rude as she pretended to be.

"If the heart is located outside the body, is it still of the body?" Megan read. "If ice is no longer solid, will it cease to be my heart? When I melt, who will drink what is left behind? Thank you."

Amid the applause, Leslie returned to her phone. Marcus's email was short. "Les," it said. "Very glad you sent this. I think of you often. Can't wait to catch up. Till soon, M."

She was torn between hating her past self—the very recently past self who had sent that email—and enjoying the surge of gratitude she felt for Marcus's response. She was skeptical of gratitude. Like humility, it was what people told you to feel after you'd been fucked over. Marcus had been awful, drugged-out and petty and selfish in the most unjustifiable ways. But the sheer reminder of his existence broadened her outlook. The world was not Missoula.

She felt something cold against the back of her neck and turned around.

"Cold Smoke?" Cal said, holding a beer. "There's a couple IPAs left, too."

"This is great," she said. "Thanks."

"Thought she was pretty good," Cal said. "Really poetic language."

"Definitely," Leslie said. She sipped her beer, which was not as cold as it had felt against her neck.

"Hey!" Cal said to a retired UM professor. "So glad you could make it, Jim."

"I'm still alive, aren't I?" Jim said. He cuffed Leslie on the shoulder, harder than was necessary. "Got a cigarette for an old man?"

"I don't think you're supposed to have any, Jim," she said.

"I'm eighty-two goddamn years old," he said. "Nobody gives a fuck what I do."

They'd been through this routine a few times. She guessed that Jim didn't know her name, but he consistently recognized her as a reliable touch for nicotine. She was only a social and emergency smoker, but she socialized and encountered emergencies with such frequency, and cigarettes in this state were so cheap, that it made sense to keep a pack on hand, if only to distinguish herself from the parasites who bummed shamelessly the minute they'd had a sip of beer. Jim was exempted from this opprobrium, of course.

"I'll come out with you," she said.

On the sidewalk, he waved her away as she tried to light his cigarette, and lit hers first with a trembling hand.

"I said I wouldn't go to any more readings," he said. "But, what the hell, it's something to do."

"Do you like Cal's writing?" she said.

"He's a good kid," he said. "Doesn't mess around too much."

This was interesting as a praiseworthy characteristic—all that most of the people Leslie knew *did* was mess around too much. She had, not quite consciously, enshrined it as something to be sought out in people, though she knew it was juvenile. Living here had brought out the hedonist in her. She'd never *not* had a tendency to drink too much, at least since she turned sixteen, but it wasn't until she got to Montana that she really began to appreciate inebriation in its various forms as an art rather than an obligation. Cal, like a decent person, considered it neither.

"Yeah, I like him," Leslie said.

"Not much of a writer," Jim said. "Nobody's perfect."

Leslie offered him a big smile in thanks for this assessment, cruel as it was. Older men loved it when she smiled at them. Jim's face, however, remained set in a scowl.

"Not that I know what the hell I'm talking about," he said hurriedly. "You write? You want to write?"

"Wish that I did, I guess," she said. "I'm one of those people with lots of *ideas*, you know?"

"Just fucking write something," he said. "Worst-case it's a piece of shit and you never show it to anybody. That's what I told my students, at least."

"Did they find that comforting?"

"A few of them wrote books. Probably no thanks to me.

Nobody really cares if you write anything. I'll be dead, at least. I don't even know you."

Leslie craned her neck around Jim to see if the homeless man was still on the sidewalk. She didn't see him. Maybe he'd made it to the parking lot of Flipper's, the bar-casino at the end of the block, which would have a legal obligation to call the police. Maybe, somehow, he'd found the energy to carry himself with something like dignity to a place that would take him in. It was hard to be entirely hopeless.

"It's always good getting your perspective, Jim," she said.

"No, it's not," he said. He tossed his lit cigarette into the street underhanded and shuffled back into the store. Leslie saw through the front window that people were sitting back down for Cal's reading. She could slip away to a bar now and be truly blitzed by the time anyone could do anything about it. Kim would come find her eventually. She'd understand, even if Leslie was unable to explain herself. The *goal* was to be unable to explain herself. Goddamn Marcus. As if he were the problem. She went back into the store. She still had three-quarters of a beer to finish.

Marcus—no, Cal, Cal—knocked the pages of his story against the lectern like a professor on TV. He was wearing the "vintage" corduroy jacket with elbow patches that Leslie had tried to convince him to throw away due to its penchant for attracting mold. Cal blamed the closet it was stored in but kept storing it there, and kept wearing it to all events that could loosely be deemed "intellectual" in nature. And, well, maybe the authentic disgustingness of the thing made it a more authentic article of clothing for him, and maybe that was what gave him the confidence he needed to read his work in front of people.

Chapter eight, the section Cal had threatened to read, turned out to be a long scene of dialogue about the nature of political corruption between the Copper King William A. Clark and his nephew Terry over cigars and brandy. "I never bought anyone who wasn't for sale," was Clark's well-worn contribution to posterity, and sure enough, Cal had him saying it within his first five lines of dialogue. It drew knowing snorts of recognition from the audience. The rest was exposition-heavy tragical-historical melodrama—"But Uncle, less than a decade ago, you promised Mother you would liquidate one-tenth of the holdings you accrued during your time in the banking industry and use that money to pay for Alexander's passage west, to start a new and better life for himself!"—and Leslie could feel the energy in the room flag with every "swirl of potent amber liquid." He did know, at least, not to read too long.

"'Father,'" Cal read with finality in his voice, "'it is half of an hour until midnight.' His daughter led him by the hand into the grand ballroom, where he would join his guests in preparing for the long-heralded new century's beginning. Thank you."

Leslie clapped hard. She really *was* proud of the way that he read, the poise he showed in front of a group, and the casual seriousness with which he carried himself. Jim was right—he didn't mess around. But to what end?

"Great job," she said to him when he'd made his way over to her. She gave him a quick kiss.

"Was it okay?" he said.

"Very commanding."

"But not like in a fascist way, right?"

"Only the tiniest bit," she said. "A little touch of fascism in the night."

"Huh," he said. "Well, I'm glad you liked it."

She squeezed his shoulder once and moved past him so that he could greet his other admirers, and then went back behind the sales desk where she knew Kim kept a bottle of Jim Beam in the bottom drawer of the filing cabinet. She took a pull from the half-full (or was it half-empty?) handle, then, before she could register the effect, took one more, holding the whiskey in her mouth for an extra unpleasant second before swallowing it. The immediate consequence was nausea, but then she felt the old pleasant warming in her brain and felt justified in her choice. All of these things that masqueraded as decisions, she knew, were really just inevitabilities.

"You, uh, drop something, Les?" Kim loomed over her.

"Yeah, I think my contact lens is in this bottle of Jim Beam," she said.

"Could you get out of there before Max sees you?" Kim said. "Come on, man."

"Feeling a little sad," Leslie said. She stood up and rested her weight on the low science-fiction shelf. "But I was feeling so good just a few minutes ago!"

"This is a good night," Kim said. "Whatever it is, you're overthinking it."

"I wish I wasn't such a jerk," Leslie said.

"Yeah, well," Kim said.

They followed the exodus out of the store and across the

Higgins Bridge. The group walked past the Wilma and the camera store where Marcus's exhibition was going to be, turned left at the creepy western expansion mural, skirted the creepy Christian coffee shop, skipped the creepy casino, and entered the Rose. The bar was dark and nearly empty, a combination of the early hour and the summer exodus of college kids.

"Shots?" Cal asked the group in general.

"Let me get this round," Leslie said. "Or at least ours. You want the special?"

"You know it," he said. Then, because he couldn't help it, "Thanks, honey."

There was a panic building in her as she ordered three sets of Jack Daniel's and Olympias, not because of the booze—though she was on her way toward being in not ideal shape on that front—but because of how little she wanted to see Cal just now. She didn't want him to know about the unprovoked sea changes in her feelings for him, but she also wasn't sure she could, in good faith, continue interacting normally. Everyone always told her that she was "moody," which she usually dismissed as, well, another way to dismiss her. But she felt the force of her mood now, the physical demands that it was making on the people around her. She was mostly mood, and only a little bit person.

She carried the three tallboys over to the table and went back for the shots. As she arrived at the bar, she saw a haggard regular dump one of her whiskeys into his own drink, then set the empty shot glass back next to the two full ones.

"What the fuck, man?" she said.

"*Excuse* me?" he said. He was accessorizing his patchy gray goatee and blotchy nose with an oversized black T-shirt.

"I saw what you did," she said. "Not cool."

"Drinks on the bar," he said, as if citing a house rule. "I see a drink on the bar, *I* don't know whose drink that is. Could be my drink, could be somebody else's. I see a drink on the bar, I figure it must be my drink. I think, *Oh, somebody bought me a drink, guess it's my lucky day.* You bought that drink? Okay. Thank you."

"You're lucky I feel guilty about a couple of other things right now," Leslie said. She collected the other two shots and brought them back to Cal and Kim.

"To a new century," Kim said.

Leslie nodded and sipped her beer. That was Kim— toasting the new century, not the last one. Kim was a wreck, too, but at least she was an optimist. She kept moving forward, maybe because she was trying to get past her family, even as she was spending all of her spare time trying to write about them. She was doing it, she would probably say, in the interest of resolving her feelings toward the past, and that was a worthy goal. Leslie worried that, for her, writing might simply be a further excuse to retreat deeper into herself, to interact with the world on the prearranged terms of her own choosing rather than the world's actual terms, whatever those turned out to be. She didn't believe that she would be able to both exist in the world of realistic expectations *and* fulfill the expectations she had for herself, expectations she had barely allowed herself to admit that she possessed. She knew, from talking to other losers, that imagining you were talented was the first step to a life of self-pity and disappointment.

"Well, so what are you going to write next?" Kim asked, interrupting some banter that Cal was having with a punk couple about an upcoming house show by a band called Fat History Month.

"I've started a couple of things," Cal said. "I kind of need to decide between the early twentieth century and, like, *way* before that. I mean, okay, I know the Revolutionary War's been done to death but it still hasn't been done, like . . . *sexy*, you know?"

"You're going to do Rev War for the ladies?" Leslie said.

"Well, for at least some of them," Cal said. "Not in a feminist way. Just, like, hey, people had lots of interesting sex back then, too. Men *and* women."

"I really can't tell if you're joking," Leslie said.

"Okay, Leslie," Kim said.

"I'm just *talking*," Leslie said. "At least I'm not bothering *you* about your shit."

"We're all admiring your restraint," Kim said.

Cal put his hand on hers from across the table.

"Les is just being the smart one," he said. "It's a tough job, but somebody has to do it."

"What does *that* mean?" Leslie said.

"I just mean you always think everything through," Cal said. "That's what I love about you. That's why we need you."

Cal's face glowed pink in the neon light of the bar's window sign, giving his affability a demonic cast. The "we" in this speech was embarrassing, worse even than the "I" and the "you."

"I think you're overestimating me," Leslie said.

She would get down to writing for real when she got home—no more putting it off. If Cal could write three lame historical novels and Marcus could become an artist, nascent or otherwise, and Kim could get on the radio, as she had last week, talking about her memoir in progress, surely she could produce something of proportionate value, or at least something not embarrassing. And if she couldn't, well, then maybe she didn't deserve to be so goddamn opinionated.

"Oh shit," Kim said, looking past Leslie. James the bartender now had the drink-stealer in a headlock from behind the bar. The haggard guy flailed his arms listlessly and kicked over a stool.

"I told you to cut it the fuck out," James said. The other guy seemed to be giving up, or passing out.

"That seems really unnecessary," Cal said.

He was probably right. And yet, she didn't feel that bad about it. How's this for identification: she wasn't sure whether she'd rather be the guy getting choked or the guy doing the choking.

"I'm going to see if I can help," Cal said. He moved toward the crowd of people who were standing around the bar not helping.

"Would you be nicer?" Kim said.

Leslie turned and gave her a slow-dawning, shrunken-head smile.

They focused their attention on the growing melee just as Cal took a kick to the nose from the flailing drunk guy. He put his hands over his face and dropped to his knees.

"Okay, *now* call the police," Kim said.

Leslie started to say, "Why me?" out of pure instinct, but caught herself. Why *not* her? She pressed the emergency button in her contact list for the first time ever as Kim moved across the room to help Cal. She tried to commit the details of the tableau to memory—the drunk's sweatpants held up, barely, by a piece of weathered rope, the usually gentle-mannered James grinning sadistically as he shouted obscenities at the man in his grip. Cal, helped to his feet by Kim, and Kim pressing a pile of cocktail napkins to his bleeding nose. When the dispatcher picked up, Leslie was pretty sure she wasn't witnessing an emergency. But since she was already on the line, she explained, as clearly as she could, what she saw. It was a first draft.

With the Christopher Kids

ON CHRISTMAS EVE I WAN-
dered around my mother's house looking for things to
wrap. For the last three days I'd been slamming doors and
doing cocaine and forgetting that it was the season of giving,
nominally because my girlfriend Melanie had left me hours
before our trip north to visit our respective families. If I
was being fair—which I wasn't—Melanie's decision made
sense: Why wait until *after* the holiday disasters to sever
ties? It was one less thing to hold against each other forever.
Downstairs, my sister Patricia hollered for scissors.

I opened the game closet and tried to find something
without too many pieces missing. First Down! NFL Chal-
lenge was unopened, but twenty years old. Warren Moon
was an Oiler. The Oilers existed. Was it nostalgic kitsch yet?
It went in the "maybe" pile. I heard Patricia pound up the
back steps with Yoshi's little dog claws clicking behind her.

"You're wrapping, yeah?" she said. "I need paper, tape,
and scissors."

"Everyone's got problems," I said.

She looked over at my gift pile: A VHS copy of *Con Air*, a dusty martini shaker, a ceramic pig.

"Maybe some of your presents can be from both of us," I said.

"Somehow that doesn't seem fair," Patricia said. My sister was in recovery and therefore disapproved of my selfish, histrionic drug binge.

"I'm doing my best," I said. Yoshi nuzzled my leg because she loved me and wanted me to be happy.

"Give me the wrapping stuff and I won't call you out on how full of shit you are," Patricia said.

When I finally came back with the things she'd asked for, Patricia was examining the underside of a massive pink conch shell that I'd found in my closet.

"'Souvenir of a lifetime, St. Kitts '96,'" she read. "Do you remember that trip?"

"No," I said.

"Me neither," she said. "Those vacations all blur together. I guess we were probably fucked up."

"We were, like, *children* in 1996," I said.

"I bet it was nice. Oh well."

I followed her downstairs but took a detour to the back deck to smoke a cigarette. There was some new snow out there that crunched under my feet in a not-hostile way. Someone had put cows in the field behind the woods, and I could hear them moaning. This was New Jersey, *Princeton*, for Christ's sake. The cows knew they were far from home.

The last night I'd spent with Melanie had been in her little house outside Durham. It rained so hard I thought the roof was going to come down on us, and when we had sex, Melanie wouldn't make a sound no matter what I did. In the morning, over pancakes, she told me she was unhappy, that she needed time to think. Then, half an hour later, while I sat drinking coffee in a diner down the street, she called and told me that, actually, she'd thought about it enough. The rain turned to snow near the fourth tollbooth in Delaware, and kept at it for the next two days.

My mother opened the porch door.

"I don't care that you're smoking," she said. "As long as it's just for now."

It was true, she didn't care. If I caught my kid smoking, I'd make him smoke a whole pack, or hang a burning cigarette around his neck for twenty-four hours like a dog that's killed a chicken.

"It's just for now," I said.

"You know, if you don't go to bed, Santa won't come."

"Ma, it's only nine-thirty."

"Not in the North Pole it isn't," she said. "How does Patricia seem to you?"

"A little on edge," I said. "But straight."

"And you?" my mother said.

I tossed my cigarette toward the trees. It landed, still lit despite the snow, in the middle of the yard. "Similar."

When I went inside, Patricia was wrapping presents at the kitchen table.

"I hate to see you like this," she said.

"Would you drive me to the train?" I said. "I want to go to New York."

"No," she said.

"Would you shoot me in the head?"

"Help me wrap this," she said. I sat down across the table from her and put Yoshi in my lap. She squirmed and whined but I held her tight.

"This is what I got Mom," Patricia said. It was a jagged chunk of shiny blue rock. "It's from Brazil. I always get her books, so I thought, *This year, make it a rock.*"

"Expensive?"

"The heart's love is priceless," she said.

Patricia was twenty-six, three years younger than me. She'd been in and out of rehab since college but seemed to have pulled it together in the last couple of years. I'd never been to rehab myself, but until recently we'd taken turns being the one with a substance problem. Now it was all up to me. She lived in New York and wrote lyrics for off-Broadway musicals; I was a freelance radio producer, which lately meant recording pieces about the Research Triangle's homeless population and then being told to send something less depressing. Tricia has always been much more talented than me, and I was proud when I wasn't furious about it. She and her writing partner were hard at work on a musical about Helen Gurley Brown, the already-overexposed editor of *Cosmopolitan*. It was a mercenary project—Tricia wasn't really into that shit—but it seemed destined for success. *Sex in the City* plus *Mad Men* plus singing till your eyes fall out.

"Can we at least go to a bar?" I said.

"Steven, it's Christmas Eve."

"Tucker's will be open," I said. A couple of Christmases

ago I'd passed out at a table in the bar and woken up on the bartender's couch, naked, but, I concluded, inviolate.

"You should think of this as an opportunity to pull yourself together," Patricia said. "You still have a choice."

"If I stay in this house one more hour I'm going to lose my fucking mind," I said. "I did a lot for you when you were in bad shape."

"When I was an *alcoholic*," Patricia said. "You are begging an *alcoholic* to take you to a bar."

"Right, but you're okay now," I said. "I'm not."

"It's called enabling," she said. "Didn't you listen on visitor's day? You've been to enough of them."

I really didn't want to go alone. I'd been having waking nightmares about Melanie, thinking she was behind me, hearing her voice in the room. And the idea of driving, after the ten-hour tear from Durham, gave me the shakes. I fled to my room and put on a Beatles record. "It won't be long, yeah. Yeah. Yeah." I cut out a line on my desk with my debit card. This was the decent stuff I'd gotten from a friend in the South, which I'd been trying to make last by alternating it with the bad stuff I'd picked up from a kid in town. I should probably mention here that I don't know anything about cocaine.

I heard a soft knock at the door and opened it a crack.

"Look, you don't need to be secretive about what you're doing in there," Patricia said.

"Sure I do."

"Well," she said. "Is it any good?"

"It's fine," I said.

"Okay, look, could I . . . could I have some?" She held out her hands like Oliver Twist.

"You shouldn't," I said.

"I know, I know," she said. "But I'd love to have just a little. It's Christmas, you know?"

She was so sweet about it, her voice gravelly and poignant. This wasn't the old junkie sis, chugging vodka out of a water bottle before dinner; this was Tricia when we were kids, asking if she could come up into the tree house. No, it was not my finest moment.

"Will you drive me to the bar?" I said.

"Definitely."

I let her in, cut the line in half, handed over the loosely rolled ten-dollar bill. She tightened it up like a pro and bent down over the desk. "Oh man, it's been a while," she said.

"Savor it," I said. "Because you aren't getting any more."

She sprawled back onto the bed. "This is all's I need."

I did mine—one more hit of cool damp cave—and put my hands on her shoulders.

"To Tucker's," I said.

"Can I have just a little *tiny* bit more?" she said. "Since I can't drink?"

Well, we'd gone this far. I cut her a line from the bad stuff.

"That one *burned*," she said. "Yuck."

When I was fourteen, I was sent off to the boarding school my father went to and found myself scared and lonely twenty-four hours a day. I was a good student but my friends were the bad kids, the ones who were smart enough not to get expelled but still spent most of their time stoned. At a school like that, where everyone was training to die of a heart attack on a yacht in the Bahamas, there was something noble about the opt-outers. I cried at night from homesickness even in my third year. I was the favorite of my first housemaster and a scourge upon my second for the same reason: I wouldn't leave him and his family alone. I could never fall asleep.

One weekend in the fall of my senior year, Tricia came up north to see me. It was against the rules, of course, but we stayed in a Marriott on Route 1 paid for by our parents, who called and told the school that they were staying with us. Tricia was sixteen and had gotten a bottle of vodka somewhere. We sat in the hotel room drinking screwdrivers and watching HBO for two days straight, eating delivery pizza and Chinese food because we were afraid of being seen by someone from school if we left the room. We came up with movie ideas and argued about the merits of Bright Eyes and drank until we threw up and then drank more. Tricia seemed to understand what my problem was even though I couldn't explain it. She made me feel better. When we said goodbye at the train station on Sunday afternoon, the thought of going back to school alone made me cry.

"You'll be home soon," Tricia said, and rubbed my back.

"I don't want to go home," I said. "I don't want anything."

"Don't be dramatic," she said.

Back at the dorm that night I finished the handle of vodka by myself and passed out on the communal bathroom floor. By some miracle my friend Landon, and not an adult or a snitch, was the one who found me, and he managed to get me back to my room. I woke up with puke in my bed and scared myself into not drinking until I went home for Thanksgiving.

And then at Thanksgiving . . . actually, that's enough.

Now, Tricia's car reeked of old cigarettes and french fries. We lit new cigarettes to cover it up. The radio was playing "Do They Know It's Christmas?"

"I wish they'd play the Italian Christmas donkey," Patricia said. "You remember the Italian Christmas donkey song?"

"It might be too racist now," I said.

"America can suck my dick," said Patricia. "This is the Wacky Races, Dick Dastardly, and Muttley. No room for moral hypocrisy here."

There was joy in me for the first time since I got dumped. We, the Christopher kids, were single and high and going to see the sad people in the bar on Christmas. We would tell them, like that angel What's-His-Name, to rejoice and be glad.

"Yo, we should pick up some candy canes," I said. "To distribute unto the drunks."

"Eh, I've got a bag of Hershey's Kisses from Halloween in the trunk," Tricia said. "No trick-or-treaters this year. As usual."

"Did you know candy canes are supposed to be shaped like shepherd's sticks?" I said. "Crooks, rather? And the red stripes are the blood of Jesus? I guess everyone knows that."

Patricia rubbed at her cheek. "My face is itchy," she said. "Does my face look weird?"

I turned on the light in the front seat and, yikes, her face *did* look a little weird. There was a fiery blotch spreading from her nose up across the side of her face.

"It's a little red," I said.

"It itches," she said. "I'm not allergic to coke. I used to do it all the time."

"Maybe you're allergic to the other stuff in it. You're not really allergic to things, are you?"

"I don't think so," she said.

I'd done plenty of that lousy batch and I felt fine.

"It'll probably go away."

I turned off the light and hoped for the best.

"Bad things always happen to me in cars," Patricia said. "Tom broke up with me when we were driving home from Cape Cod. Then I crashed my car and had to go to rehab. Cars are a real problem area for me."

"Trains are good," I said. "I'd *live* on a train if I could."

We were at the parking lot of the bar, which looked dark but open, with a few beat-up cars out front.

"Okay, my face is officially fucking on fire," Patricia said. She turned on the light and flipped down the driver's-side mirror. Her face was a mess. The right side was so swollen that her eye was almost closed.

"Oh shit, Stevie," she said. "I think I need to go to the hospital."

"Maybe the bar will have some antihistamines or something," I said. "Don't worry. If something really bad was going to happen it would've happened already."

I patted her on the shoulder and she jerked away. I hustled into the bar and immediately felt better in the bleach-smelling dimness. The front area was a liquor store, half lit and empty, and a couple of guys were slumped at the bar in the back of the room. Maud the bartender was looking up at a TV playing *It's a Wonderful Life*. It was the scene where Jimmy Stewart abandons his new wife to calm the run on the bank. The blonde whose name I could never remember was standing behind Maud wearing an apron. As if they needed a waitress tonight. Maybe she had a bad family life and wanted to be my new girlfriend?

"Maud, I came to celebrate the birth of Christ with you, but I wonder if you have any antihistamines?"

"What a nice tradition this is!" she said.

"My sister's having an allergic reaction," I said. "She's feeling anxious about it."

"Aw, the little drunk?" she said. "That's a shame. I think I have some Advil."

"Let's give it a chance," I said. "And some ice in a cup and some water?" And. "And a couple shots of vodka?"

As she got the stuff an old guy at the bar turned to me. "Crap Christmas," he said.

"I've got some candy in the car," I said. "You like Hershey's Kisses?"

He worked his grizzled jaws like he already had that chocolate in his mouth.

"Don't you have a family to bother?" he said.

I took down my shots and gathered the supplies from Maud. "Couch is free, kid," she said.

"Did you expect me to *pay* for it?" I said.

"The drinks aren't."

"On my tab," I said. "And tip yourself extra holiday bucks!" I didn't have a tab.

In the car, Tricia was leaning back in her seat with her eyes closed. She was mutating before my eyes. "Steven?" she croaked. "You need to drive me to the hospital."

"Take this Advil," I said. "You'll feel better."

Going to the hospital would be the worst bad thing. It would be bright-lit and filled with terrible Christmas decorations and one sad paper menorah. It would be another unhappy installment of the Christopher kids story: the time they spent Christmas in the hospital from bad drugs. It would take its place next to the time Patricia passed out backstage at one of our father's speeches, the time we missed our aunt's funeral because we were too stoned to drive, the time Patricia broke the first-floor windows of our father's girlfriend's house, which was also the time she found out that our father had a girlfriend. Couldn't this be the time that Patricia's immune system saved the day?

"My throat is swelling," she said, and she sounded awfully convincing. I raised an Advil up to her lips but she shook her head and closed her eyes, laid her head back against her headrest in defeat. Fine.

"Didn't they move the hospital?" I said.

"It's a new one," Tricia said. "It's off 95 by the West Trenton exit."

"Well, I guess it'd be good to know what the new scene is like," I said. "The more you know, right?"

I got out and guided her around to the passenger seat. I clanged the driver's seat back and jammed out of the lot. She started wheezing in a spooky way so I gunned it to eighty on the highway and rolled down my window to let the cold winter air fill the car and drive out the bad spirits. I thought about calling our father but what was he going to say? Go to the hospital. Then he'd show up there and I'd have to deal with him.

"Okay, Trish?" I said.

No answer. I looked over and her eyes were closed, but I could hear her rasping.

I slowed down to follow the signs guiding the way to the hospital and parked in an emergency parking zone, then dragged Patricia out of the car and shuffle-stepped her to the door. Her face looked like a half-deflated basketball and her breaths had gotten shallow.

The lady at the front desk—mountainous, sleepy—told me to have a seat.

"Shit's on the verge here," I said. "Look at her."

"Sir," she said. "Everything is on the verge of something."

The whole gang of waiting-room people was there— a wild-eyed white guy with a mustache and a chest wound, a half-asleep black man who seemed to be wearing a floral bedsheet, an Asian woman exhaustedly clutching a comatose child. I declined feeling like a part of the cosmic web that contained them. If they were anything like me, they had brought this on themselves. But I was wrong about the Christmas decorations: there weren't any. Tricia took slow, labored breaths until a nurse came and put her in a wheelchair.

"It's going to be okay," I said.

She wheezed something that sounded like "blood traffic."

I sat there and looked at pictures of Melanie on my phone—Melanie holding a pumpkin, Melanie next to a stranger's miniature husky—until I'd scrolled back to the beginning of our relationship, represented by the dim interior shots of my apartment in Durham before I rented it. Then I turned my phone off, in case my mother woke up and tried to call me.

"Christopher?" the nurse said, an hour later. "Brother? Would you come back with me, please?"

I followed her through the swinging doors. Patricia was in a bed with railings, hooked up to an IV, eyes closed. A gawky young guy in a white coat was standing next to the bed. A doctor, I guess.

"So, Steven?" he said. "Your sister's had a serious allergic reaction, probably to something in the cocaine she was using."

"Right," I said. "How is she?"

"She's stable," the doctor said. "We'll see how things look in the morning."

"Can't we go sooner?" I said. "Like, now? It's Christmas."

"Are you a drug user, Steven?" the doctor said.

"On occasion. Recreationally, I mean."

"Well, you might want to think about that. If your sister hadn't come to see us, she could have ended up in a very bad place."

"Dead?"

"Let's just say it wouldn't have been good."

"No, seriously," I said. "I'd like to know the full fucking extent of my negligence."

The doctor kept a patient smirk on his face.

"Sure, she could have died," the doctor said. "Lucky for her she has such a responsible brother."

Well, that triggered my despair, which I have a real problem with.

"I'm sorry," I said, to Patricia who couldn't hear me, and to the doctor, who didn't care. I thought of our mother, asleep at home, soon to be confronted with this. She'd try, with good reason, to get Patricia to quit her show and go back into treatment, which she wouldn't do. I sat in the padded chair next to her bed and watched her breathe, each breath like an accusation. I fell asleep sitting there.

At seven she woke up.

"Oh *fuck*," she said.

"How do you feel?" I said.

"Terrible. I feel terrible."

"God, I'm so glad you're all right."

"Well, I'm a junkie," she said. "Have you talked to Mom?"

"I thought that could be your job," I said.

"Jesus, she's probably out of her mind. Give me my bag."

She pulled her phone out and dialed.

"Hi, Mom? I'm okay. Yes, I'm okay, I promise . . ."

I walked to the waiting room and chugged a Diet Coke from the vending machine. Christmas morning.

My mother arrived a half hour later. She had dark circles under her eyes and she was wearing a bright red sweater with an enormous green bow on the front, a joke Christmas present from last year that had apparently been appropriated into unironic holiday wear. The doctors told us they wanted Tricia to stay in the hospital for a few more hours. I got my mother some coffee from a machine and sat down next to her.

"Do you ever think about how I'm going to feel when you finally kill yourselves?" she said.

"It was just bad luck," I said. "This is the last time for this. We're done now."

"Why do you even come home?" she said.

"For you?" I said.

"Well, thanks, Steven. Really."

"I'll be gone soon enough," I said. I was trying for ominous but I didn't make it past petulant.

At noon I told my mother I was going home and instead drove into town blasting Wu-Tang's *36 Chambers* with my windows down, drawing glances of pitying forbearance from the strolling families of Princeton. I did this until the album started over for the third time, at which point my hands were so numb that it was a struggle just to turn the music off. I pulled into the empty parking lot by the bad sushi place.

There were so many choices: I could ask my father for money, drive west, change my life. Stick to weed. Send cards on birthdays and holidays. Learn to love myself and, eventually, someone nice and low-pressure. Raise chickens. Forgo procreation. Show up secretly to the premiere of Tricia's first Broadway show and sit in the back, waiting until after the standing ovation to reveal myself. Be forgiven.

An hour later I sat in the living room with Patricia and my mother, unwrapping presents. I gave my mother the shell I'd found in the house.

"I remember this trip," my mother said. "This is a weird present, Steven."

"Patricia and I can't remember it," I said. "We wanted you to remind us."

I tried to catch my sister's eye but she was looking at her lap.

"You didn't go," my mother said. "Your father and I went for our anniversary. It was nice. Pretty sunsets. You know, a Caribbean island."

Well, it was better to have never been there, maybe, than to have forgotten it.

Patricia handed my mother her next present and she unwrapped it.

"A rock," she said. "How thoughtful."

An hour later, I knocked on the door of what used to be Tricia's bedroom. She was sitting on her bed, cross-legged, reading a Jerry Lee Lewis biography.

"I'm heading out," I said. "Gonna stay with Sam in D.C. for a while."

"Now, *there's* a good influence," she said.

"Is there somewhere you'd rather I fuck off to and die?"

She went back to looking at her book.

"You're not going to die."

Tricia's walls had once been covered in ugly magazine ads, drunken Polaroids, Clash posters. Not even the ceiling had been spared her chaos. My mother had turned it into a guest room years ago, so now bland flower prints were our only witnesses.

"I guess we'll see," I said.

She put the book facedown on the bed and hugged her legs to her chest.

"Don't die, though," she said. "Really."

And I didn't. After getting kicked out of Sam's house, I sublet a dirty furnished apartment across the street from the University for the Deaf. I got a nearly full-time job working on a janky local-politics show, splicing together sound bites from city council members into unconvincing denials of corruption. Funny: it made me feel better about my life, and gave me less time to drink. I even handled a few objectively harrowing OkCupid dates without spiraling into the void.

One night, while I was having some whiskey—out of a glass, okay, with ice—and watching an incomprehensible late-night talk show, there was a knock on my door. I knew it was Patricia before I opened it. She was skeletal and green, her eyes unfocused and deep in her skull. She wore a huge camping backpack that hulked around the edges of her torso.

"Okay, I'm here," she said.

"What happened?" I said.

She stepped into the apartment. Her eyes lingered on the ratty plaid-upholstered armchairs and the wood-paneled entertainment system.

"This place is pretty sweet," she said.

"There's a little bit of a mold thing," I said modestly.

I gave her a hug, felt how frail her limbs and shoulders were.

"I know I look like shit," she said. "But it's because I'm actually not drinking now and my body's, like, really not reacting well to that."

"Are you sure?" I said.

"About which part?"

"Any of it," I said. "You look like you should be in a fucking hospital."

"Can I put my bag down?" she said.

"What am I going to do, kick you out?" I said it like I was furious with her, though I wasn't. I was trying to wake her up, maybe, or keep myself from falling back into the old dream. She sloughed off her bag and sat down gently in one of the chairs, crossing her legs like she was waiting to be served tea. She stared at the sweating glass of whiskey on the coffee table.

"I'm working on a lot of things," she said. "I think, maybe, we need to exercise some collective willpower."

"What's going on with your show?" I said. "What are you doing with yourself?"

"Everything," she said evenly. "Is on. Hold."

She was still fixated on the whiskey. I carried it into the bathroom, drank down half of it, and poured the rest in the sink. The ice bunched around the drain and I knew, obviously, that it was just a symbolic gesture. But so was a peace treaty, right? So was a funeral.

I set the empty glass on the coffee table and sat down in the wooden chair across from my sister.

"How about something to eat?" I said.

She rolled her eyes, a slow, glitchy process, and shuddered.

"Give me a second," she said.

I leaned back in my chair. There was no rush. I mean, it wasn't like I had any food.

Childhood, Boyhood, Youth

THEY HAD FINISHED READ-
ing *War and Peace*, and now they were celebrating their
triumph at a Russian supper club in Brighton Beach.
There were twelve of them seated at the long table ("Just
like what's-his-name, minus what's-his-name," Kyla said
brightly), and, well, Derek assumed that at least half of
them had probably finished *War and Peace*. Or, fine: he
imagined it was safe to say that, on the whole, the table had
at least started reading *War and Peace*.

Derek had made it to within a hundred pages of the end,
though he had admittedly skimmed a little down the stretch.
He knew that Pierre and Natasha got together, which had
begun to seem structurally inevitable at some point—in ap-
proximately ten thousand pages there were only about five
characters—though it was somewhat psychologically im-
probable. He also wasn't totally clear on what a samovar was.

He'd been proven wrong in his interpretations of the text
at every turn over the eight months they'd spent reading and

discussing the book, his theories and analyses shot down by better, or at least more confidently, educated members of the group. Some of them had gone to Yale and others to Harvard, and he'd developed a handy cheat to remember which was which. The Harvard kids acted mildly embarrassed when he said something dumb, sometimes even waiting until after the session to correct him on his political or geographical ignorance. The ones from Yale made sure to keep the humiliation public and, if possible, prolonged.

In one of their first meetings, Derek had suggested that Tolstoy showed a grudging respect for Napoleon, or was at least willing to acknowledge his world-historic importance, even though he was the enemy.

"That's *completely* the opposite of true," a tall, dark-haired man named Jonathan said. "Tolstoy *despised* Napoleon, and thought the whole *idea* of historical significance was nonsense. Do you have *any* examples?"

Derek had glanced around the room for support, but even Thomas, his roommate, whom he had invited specifically to back him up in moments like this, only stared down at the massive open book in his lap.

"Just . . . in the prose itself, I guess," Derek said. "The prose about Napoleon just feels like it has an air of respect to it."

"Well, does his prose ever seem *dis*respectful to you?" Jonathan said, peering down his nose through invisible reading glasses.

"To be fair, it *is* translated," Violet said. "I don't imagine *any* of us can really comment on the *prose* style very accurately."

They all, consciously or not, transferred their gazes toward Pyotr, who had moved to the States when he was seven and was ostentatiously reading the book in his Russian parents' Soviet-era multivolume set.

"Sorry friends, my literary analysis isn't strong enough in either language to gauge, ah, *respectfulness*," he said amiably. "Plus, I didn't even know Napoleon was in this section. I was too busy the last couple of weeks to keep up."

Pyotr was in law school at Columbia, a sudden turn he'd taken after two years of working on a comp lit Ph.D. in which he'd planned to focus on Italo Svevo and Joseph Roth. Derek assumed that Pyotr must have been extremely intelligent, given these pursuits, but at that point he had yet to contribute anything to the reading group other than encouraging nods and smiles. Now, after what felt like nearly a lifetime later, Pyotr sat kitty-corner from Derek at the supper club, bantering with their bald, sinister waiter in, presumably, Russian. Pyotr had attended maybe half of the group's sessions, and Derek guessed that he might have read the least amount of *War and Peace* of anyone, with the likely exception of Leslie, who argued fiercely and cheerfully about the book month after month despite clearly having only the most glancing familiarity with its contents. She *had* apparently read enough to draw a faint mustache on her upper lip upon arrival at the restaurant, in honor, she said, of the Little Princess.

Derek mostly admired her impudence, though sometimes he wished she would admit analytical defeat a little bit sooner in the group's exchanges so that they could all move on to something more, well, reality-based. Vivek, clearly at least half in love with Leslie (*most* clearly when his part-ner Nell was not in attendance), indulged even her most scattershot theories—maybe Prince Andrei *was* gay—with what seemed to be the moral authority bestowed on him by the group. He'd had a local organizational role of some import, apparently, in the Obama campaign, and, though now only in his second year of medical school, he'd appar-ently contributed not insignificantly, in his telling at least, to "strategy and messaging" around the Affordable Care Act. Which, given what a clusterfuck *that* was, shouldn't necessarily have accrued such favor to him, Derek thought. Like a jerk.

The reading group (*not* book club) had begun meeting in January, two months after the midterm elections that had, as they could not yet know, swept the Democrats out of congressional power for the next almost-decade, and Vivek was treated with the mild deference of someone who had re-cently suffered the death of a somewhat important relative, a great-uncle, maybe, or adult cousin. There were no Re-publicans among them, of course, but there was some range in the degree to which politics was central to their lives, running the gamut from the socialists associate-editing a newish journal of "literature and ideas" to Thomas, who voted for Democrats, presumably, if he voted, but also went to church, exercised regularly, and worked for an interna-tional bank. Derek had felt in himself a recent, emerging de-sire for political commitment (like Larkin in the abandoned church, but for economic justice?), though he hadn't acted on it. He didn't enjoy going to protests, and he didn't want to be in one of the Marxist reading groups whose membership overlapped significantly with this one. Maybe he would ask Vivek if there was anything he could do for 2012, though he feared that would prove less than life-changing. Hope had pulled off the big win once; what could the next election be but a crowd-pleasing but redundant sequel?

Violet, who had invited him into the group in the first place, was directly across the table from him. She had been, until quite recently, a fellow assistant of his at the august, maybe dying small magazine where he still worked. Now she had a job as a web editor at a more prestigious, definitely not dying, publication, and Derek saw her mostly at parties or at book club (*reading group*), though she did text him sometimes, often five or six messages in a row, to complain about some obstinate writer who wouldn't take edits or, more pointedly, at least in Derek's mind, about the ridiculousness of the date she'd been on the night before. Sometimes—*good days*, as he thought of them, with some embarrassment—this would lead to hours of nearly unbroken texting between them, during which Derek's work, to put it lightly, suffered. He'd carry out his tasks in a haze of composition, mentally rearranging the punctuation in his responses until they had achieved a perfect balance of intelligence and spontaneity. He could hardly remember what they'd been discussing even minutes after the flurries ended—the editor who'd gotten fired over an ill-judged headline, the Arab Spring, the inadequacy of birth-control options—but the exchanges left him humming with pleasure and immediately starving for more. Most times, the conversation would go cold after one or two volleys, with Derek feeling phantom buzzes against his hip, checking his phone every few minutes for the rest of the day hoping she might have decided, after a few hours of serious contemplation, to reply to, "Ha, crazy! What do you think he meant???"

Derek wasn't delusional enough to think it likely that Violet had any interest in him beyond their already loosely bound friendship, but he was happy to be the recipient of her excess feelings, thoughts, whatever. She was two years older than him and had only predated him at their publication by a matter of months. But somehow this small gulf placed her on a radically distinct plane of experience in his eyes, as alien to his as when he'd been an eighth-grader watching through the chain-link fence bordering the sports fields as the members of the high school soccer team smoked cigarettes and impugned each others' manhood. He knew that this didn't have to be the case—he felt on equal footing with, if severely annoyed by the condescension of, most of the members of the reading group—but he still couldn't help but think of Violet as morally and intellectually superior. And he felt the latter to be true despite what seemed her studied (or unstudied?) indifference to the standard intellectual markers and pretensions of the time. She claimed to be unironically engrossed by the celebrity Internet, and she paid to see romantic comedies and horror sequels that could only be sociologically interesting, if at all. She chewed gum at all hours, sometimes *while* smoking cigarettes. And yet she was friends with *people*. The pop music critic for the *Times*. The Booker-winning young Scottish novelist who taught at NYU. She acted as though she'd gotten her fancy job by accident, as though one could just sort of pick up the phone and find oneself editing . . . *whoever* the next day.

And maybe, he thought, if one was smart and cool enough (and, all right, went to Yale), one could.

"Okay, *least* valuable player," Violet was saying across the table to the three or four people who were listening.

"Everyone was *so* valuable," Kyla said, to Derek's left. She was very thin and very drunk and Derek wondered if it was too early to suggest she skip the next round of the already innumerable vodka shots they'd downed from the handles on ice in the center of the table. "You can't attach *value* to *people*," she continued when no one responded. "Tolstoy? Gandhi? Hello?"

"I was going to nominate Ben, because he only came once and spilled wine all over his book," Violet said. "But maybe that's 'not nice' and we should 'respect all members of the group no matter how tertiary and useless.'"

"Can I at least be the least valuable regular attendee, then?" Leslie said. "Do I get a prize? I didn't learn nothing, I swear!"

"Only a man can be least valuable," Violet said. "We see right through that mustache, missy. In addition, I hereforth nominate Derek for rookie of the year."

"Aren't we *all* rookies?" Kyla said. "Isn't this the first and, God willing, only year of this?"

"No, and no," Violet said. "Derek is just a boy and he's from some terrible state that starts with an *I*, and yet he is a *leading* editorial assistant *and* he attended every meeting."

Derek was actually from South Jersey but it was close enough in spirit, and he was ninety percent sure Violet actually knew where he was from. Eighty percent. Also, he was a pretty bad assistant.

Vivek tousled Derek's hair, emitting a strangulated howl that one had to assume was intended as celebratory. "As a commander in the Muslim Brotherhood of Hussein Obama, I hereby second this nomination for world's cutest rookie of the year dot-com," he said. "Your T-shirt is hereby in the mail."

Derek leaned over to see what his sworn rival Jonathan thought of all this silliness, but he was deep in conversation with Thomas at the end of the table. Jonathan was working on a piece, he'd been telling them all relentlessly, about how economics was fake, and Thomas, in his blessed, mildly autistic way, had been contradicting him at every opportunity. Now Thomas appeared to be drawing a chart of some kind on the, well, directly on the tablecloth. The place served vodka like tap water—surely it had seen worse.

"Fifty K for a verse, no album out," Derek toasted, raising his half-full glass.

Those who had been following the conversation took down their shots, or pretended to.

Prominent in Derek's mind was the fact that Violet had recently gotten back together with her ex-boyfriend, or was at the very least sleeping with him again. The ex, semi-ex, whatever, was in his mid-thirties, a published novelist and assistant professor at Brooklyn College named Morgan Calder. (The name sounded made up. Did writers still change their names?) Presently Violet was focused on her lap, a half smile fixed on her face. Derek assumed she was texting. The guy sounded, despite the likelihood of arrogance and unkindness suggested by his credentials, normal and decent; if anyone was mistreating anyone it was prob-

ably Violet, who seemed to fluctuate weekly between devotion and utter indifference. Not that Derek had an excess of
sympathy for the guy.

He'd been on a few dates lately himself. After spending
most of college with Allie (who had gone to Berlin to "check
things out" and decided there that Derek, and New York as
a whole, no hard feelings, had not been bringing out her best
self for quite some time), he'd found himself in a series of
months-long relationships, each of which had ended when
one or the other party had mercifully taken the karmic
blow and acknowledged that, though things between them
were rarely less than pleasant, there did not appear to be a
pressing need for continued brunches, cocktails, oral sex,
etc. Presently he was spending occasional time with Saman-
tha, the current roommate of a college friend. She was calm,
zaftig, often dressed like a cowboy. She worked for the Department of Transportation in some capacity, and people
thought it was funny to pretend to be mad at her when they
arrived late for something because of the subway. She had
the decency to pretend she thought this was amusing. The
second night he slept over at her place she asked if he wanted
to tie her up—and he did!—though he was more enthusiastic
than effective. She made fun of him for not knowing about
knots and safe words. He agreed that it would be useful to
have complicated sex skills, but he got the sense that both of
them were thinking these would be used elsewhere.

It *was* something of an advantage, he'd realized when
he moved to New York, to be thought of as a hick on occasion. It gave him time to figure things out, which he
suspected everyone, even those born on the Upper East

Side or wherever, would appreciate having if they allowed it to themselves. He was from a township adjacent to Cape May and other self-consciously quaint shore towns, but dull and inland enough to be cheap and ugly. He'd worked beach jobs in the summer, spent weekend nights in Wildwood. His description of the Cowtown Rodeo, which his family had attended every year of his existence, was probably what had stuck the idea of the Midwest, ironic or otherwise, in Violet's head.

"What, do they do the rodeo in, like, a parking lot?" she'd said as they made their ritualistic trudge to the Hudson River on one of their work breaks, before she'd gotten too big for book reviews.

"South Jersey can get pretty country, man," he said. "These guys were legit cowboys. I never even heard that ridiculous quote Jersey accent until I got to NYU."

"Don't worry, I believe your life was ridiculous," Violet said.

She had been born in New York (the Upper *West* Side), lived in England as a child, returned to the city as a teenager, then off to New Haven. He forgave her for all of this, obviously, because she paid attention to him.

When he'd gone home to see his family for the Fourth of July weekend, he brought his copy of *War and Peace*, reading it on the bus between bursts of motion sickness.

"Is that actually as good as it's supposed to be?" his mother said when he got to the house. "I always wondered if it was really, you know, the *best* book."

His mother taught middle school English, and when she wasn't reading *To Kill a Mockingbird* for the thousandth time she gravitated toward novels with ominous lines from nursery rhymes in their titles. (She appeared to be halfway through *And Jill Came Tumbling After*.)

"Believe the hype, Ma," Derek said.

"No one invited *me* to the book club," she said. "I think you could *use* a little age diversity in there. Does anybody ever admit it when they don't understand something? Or is everybody too cool and serious for that?"

"It's pretty easy to read on, like, a sentence level," he said. "There's a lot of pseudo-philosophy, though, and most people admit that they can't really follow it. Or, I mean, I think people actually *do* understand, or would if they tried, but it's kind of the convention to throw up your hands at the essay parts. *I* kind of think those are the best parts, honestly."

"Well, maybe I'll get the audiobook for my walks."

"That'd be a lot of walks, Ma."

The whole family went to Wildwood for the fireworks, his parents and sister and grandmother all piled into the aging SUV, parking a mile from the boardwalk to avoid paying exorbitant lot fees. They walked past the ancient pastel-colored motels, the narrow apartment buildings where old, shirtless men in plastic chairs smoked cigars and eyed the passing humans with naked skepticism. The crowds grew thicker as they approached the boardwalk, and they folded themselves in among the intricately tattooed Hispanic men with little girls on their shoulders, the sobbing white children dragged toward the ocean by sunburned mothers. The sounds of chaos were imminent: electronic clanging from thousands of desperate games, muffled exhortations with

Eastern European accents through cheap microphones, the brief crash of the wooden coaster and its seconds of audible screams. It was a nightmare of the past, annually renewed with T-shirts bearing the past year's catchphrases. He went regardless of whether it was, what, *compatible* with how he now imagined himself. He wished sometimes that his family were far away or unkind enough that he could justify not returning to this primordial slop, which, no matter how hard he tried for it not to, left him dizzy with despair every time he was re-immersed in it.

And yet it felt necessary somehow, not because he believed in the importance of family or tradition or any of that other insidious conservative bullshit, but more in the name of research, maybe, the ongoing investigation into his feelings that he was conducting with what felt like increasing rigor and depth. He didn't think he was getting *smarter*, necessarily, despite all the Tolstoy and his recent timid line-editing of elderly Nobel laureates. It felt instead like the more he learned, the less he was able to assimilate into a coherent, what, *body of knowledge*? He was frustrated by the gap between what he knew he was capable of and what he could actively process. But, he thought, he would get older, and learn more, and assimilate more, and at some point he'd have something resembling wisdom, he hoped. And then he and the surviving members of the *War and Peace* reading group would sometimes remember over the years how insistently clever and intense they'd all been when they were twenty-four, twenty-five, twenty-six, working for people more important than they were and, some more consciously than others, building these little, yuck, *networks* for future success by hosting each other in their apartments around the city for the better part of a year under the pretext of discussing Russian literature.

Derek's turn to host, in mid-September, had been a source of near-constant anxiety after they'd each signed up for a slot at the first meeting. The overriding concern was, of course, that no one would come, followed very closely by the fear that *everyone* would come and he wouldn't have enough chairs, snacks, etc., and that they would all be too warm and crowded in his narrow apartment. His third biggest concern was that an average number of people would come and, having neither the chaos of an overcrowded room nor the immense pity attendant upon a nearly empty one to distract their attention, they would focus on the starkly suboptimal state of his decorating, housekeeping, and general life-maintenance abilities. He lived in a third-floor walkup in Bed-Stuy that he shared with Thomas, who kept his room fastidiously clean but refused "moral responsibility" for the common room due to what he felt was an unfair rent split (even though his room was three times larger than Derek's), and Arian, a nervous, rarely seen young Persian man who claimed to be a software developer. Two weeks before the meeting, Thomas announced that he was going to be out of town for a conference, which he had surely known about for far longer than he was admitting. Derek had suspected he might pull something like this, and tried to chalk it up to Thomas's legitimately crippling—if somewhat, it had to be said, conveniently deployed—social anxiety. Derek just had regular anxiety, which in this case happened to be triggered by social expectations.

So he did his best to clean the house, scrubbing at the filthy baseboards, vacuuming inefficiently with a monstrous Oreck he'd found deep in a closet, gathering up months' worth of magazines and dumping them in the recycling box (though he would wait until he'd had a chance to go through them again one more time before actually putting them outside for collection). He sent two self-deprecating reminder emails to the group and bought hummus and Brie and baguettes and two cases of decent beer, then sat staring at the pages they were supposed to be discussing while he waited for it to be seven o'clock. Leslie arrived first, at 7:15, looking stoned and bashful, clutching her gigantic paperback to her chest like she was going to use it to try to stop a bullet.

"Oh no, did I restore your faith in humanity?" she said, peering into the empty apartment. "I swear I just came to be polite, not because I like or respect you."

"More beer for us, am I right?" Derek said. He assumed she would understand that his reliance on a tedious cliché was intentional.

"Oh, I'll *drink* your beer," Leslie said. "Just don't expect me to know anything about *Spy vs. Spy* over here. Maybe I need a different translation. One with pictures, and sound. A *movie*, you might call it."

"We could try to find the Audrey Hepburn one online if nobody else shows up," Derek said.

"Ooo, I'm gonna tell Violet you suggested we *watch a movie* together," Leslie said. "She is gonna *freak*."

"Or we could just skip right to seven minutes in heaven."

"More like twenty seconds I bet," she said, her head deep in the refrigerator. "Is this pizza slice, like, up for grabs?"

A perfectly unremarkable number of people eventually showed up, Vivek and Kyla and Jonathan and, hallelujah, Violet, who glanced around at the bare walls and deeply gouged wood floors and declared the place "not as bad as I'd assumed it would be." Jonathan went on and on about Irving Berlin and hedgehogs, while Derek tried to look at Violet without being obvious about it. At one point, while Leslie and Vivek argued about *Watch the Throne*, he accidentally caught Violet's eye, and she performed an extremely slow-motion and detailed pantomime of vomiting down the front of her shirt. He *wished* Leslie would try to incite jealousy in her. It certainly couldn't be any worse than this semi-public but unacknowledged *pining*.

Now, at the long table in the supper club, no one seemed to be eating enough pickled herring or creamed anything to keep up with their vodka intake. ("Where is the horse-flesh?" Kyla yelled.) Violet had tripped coming back from the bathroom, and might have sprawled headfirst into the table but for the intervention of the maybe-not-so-sinister-after-all waiter, who caught her delicately by the waist and guided her into her seat without making a show of it. These things happened, after all, when aristocrats gathered. Violet acted as though she'd expected the waiter to be there, flashing him a polite, thank-you-for-your-service smile before resuming her conversation with Pyotr. Derek had too much faith in her to be worried. If she was drunk, she intended to be drunk, and would enjoy herself accordingly. But, also, he'd keep an eye out just in case it seemed like she was about to fall over again.

He'd moved down to the corner of the table to talk to

Patrick, who was the lead singer of a rock band that had just received a devastating negative review on a popular website. Derek was existentially unnerved by the unfairness of it. Patrick was sweet and funny, and everyone who heard his music loved it, and yet now some asshole had endangered his whole possible career because his album didn't meet some nonsensical standard of *originality*, as defined by a critic whose sense of history didn't extend any further back than David Bowie's third album. As if originality even existed. He realized this was a rich position to take, as someone who edited (assisted in the editing of) reviews of various degrees of negativity, and he had already written a couple of less-than-positive ones himself, though they were for obscure-enough venues that he was confident he hadn't exactly derailed anyone's ambitions. It was wrong, he knew, that the reason he was opposed to this particular bad review was that it was *Patrick*, a person who was already so sufficiently self-effacing that he didn't need a website to tell him that he should dislike his own work. The solution, Patrick was telling him now, was not to take things personally. One needed, he had discovered, to let one's work be as the seagull over the ocean, drifting on currents and squawking horribly, unencumbered by the dull perspectives of the beachgoers on the distant shore.

"Huh," Derek said.

"Yeah, I guess I've been thinking about it too much," Patrick said.

"The *real* question," Kyla was saying loudly, trying to get the table's attention, "is what are we going to read *next*?"

"Let's read what's-his-name's book!" Leslie said. "Violet's boyfriend! And then we can have him come and tell him about it to his *face*!"

"Yes," Jonathan said. "Yes. Yes. A hundred times yes."

"Have *you* read his books, Violet?" Kyla said.

"Ummmmm," Violet said. She took a long, stagey sip of water. "Officially? Yes."

"But among dear friends with extremely good taste and a commitment to hard truths?" said Leslie.

"*If* I were to find myself communicating with such an audience, I might feel obliged to admit that I have not yet completed the works under discussion."

"*Yet?*" Jonathan said. "So you're still, uh, anticipating completion?"

"Well, if the fucker doesn't start learning how to *text back within an appropriate time span*, then I think I'm going to consider myself off the hook, like, in general. He's thirty-five, not *one hundred*, it shouldn't be that hard. And also, no, we are not reading his books, that is not appropriate."

"It sounds to me like you just set the stage for Secret Book Club," Vivek said. "Anyone who doesn't not want to be in Secret Book Club, say nothing."

They pondered this construction, chose to remain silent. Derek felt a surge of hope. She hadn't even *finished* his *books*? Not even one of them? Surely they were not destined for a long and happy life together. He could wait. In the meantime he would read and write more, lose some weight, buy better clothes, get a nicer apartment . . .

Suddenly the restaurant dimmed, and green laser lights glowed through fog at the front of the room. A man in a tuxedo emerged from the alien smoke, flanked by women wearing green leotards and feathered headdresses. "Copacabana" began playing at a nerve-shattering volume, and the tuxedoed man sang heartily in Russian-accented English. The floor show had begun.

Nearly three hours and dozens of songs, magic tricks, and unconsummated stripteases later, Derek, Violet, and Kyla were sharing a car back toward their respective neighborhoods. Derek was in a borderland of drunkenness, his memory of the night already growing disordered, but not drunk enough to be fully without care. He was, in other words, less drunk than Kyla and Violet, which meant that he felt somewhat responsible for their well-being. Kyla was, for the most part, passed out, lifting her head from Violet's shoulder to mumble what seemed to be nonsensical driving directions. Violet was more active in her inebriation; she had, for the past ten minutes, been telling a story about an art opening she'd gone to in which she'd accidentally insulted Kim Gordon by complaining about a dress that she hadn't realized she'd designed. Or something. It was hard to follow.

"Do you know where Kyla lives?" he said, twisting around from the front seat at what felt like a reasonable stopping point in the story.

"Oh, yeah," she said. "It's . . . well, actually no. No, no, I do not. Whose address did we give him?"

"I think yours," he said. "Doesn't she live near you?"

"Hmmm." She nudged Kyla, then, receiving no response, elbowed her in the side. "Hey, Ky, where do you even live?"

"Twelve-twenty-six North Lowry Boulevard, Spring-field, Massachusetts 01129," she said in a low monotone.

"I'll take her to my place," she said. "Hangovers are better together. And if either of us dies, everyone can just blame it on the other one."

"That's terrible," Derek said. "Do you feel all right?"

"I feel the weight of the world. Right exactly on the tippy top of my head."

"Huh. Have you heard from, uh, Morgan?"

"Honestly, no," she said. She sighed heavily. "He's . . . whatever. Life is long and full of terror. I don't have time for this kind of thing right now."

"I'm gonna read his book," Derek said. "Which one's shorter?"

"There's so many people to mee-eet," she sang, badly, to the melody of an Elvis Costello song that wasn't play-ing. "They only slide you up with nothing when you think you're havin' fu-un."

"I guess the only thing we could really read next is Proust. Then we could be in book group for the rest of our lives, basically."

"You just wanna keep hanging out with mee-eee," she kept singing. "But you don't want to admit it 'cause you're a little bi-it awk-ward."

"In Illinoidiana, we keep our feelings deep inside and never tell anyone about them," he said. "It's how we protect ourselves from Yankee cruelty."

She gently moved Kyla's head from her shoulder to the window, and then leaned forward to the cab's open partition.

"You're really quite a goofball," she said.

"Well, sure," he said.

"I mean, really. Quite. Here's good!" The car pulled to a stop. "Help me get Kyla upstairs?"

But Kyla managed to remove herself from the car under her own power, and Derek simply followed the two of them uselessly, like a third friend pretending to help move a couch. He'd been to Violet's once before, when she'd hosted the group, and it was as he'd re-created it in his head—a long, bike-choked hallway giving way to a large, black-and-white-tiled kitchen, then emptying out into a well-appointed sitting room, complete with Cy Twombly and Christopher Wool exhibition posters and a large television. The bedroom, presumably, was behind one of those doors off the hallway. He would not see it tonight. There would come a time when they would be equals, he reminded himself.

Kyla somnambulated to the couch, stretched across it like a cat, and fell immediately unconscious. Violet threw herself into the giant armchair and curled her legs under her dress.

"You've been a lovely audience, and I hope we passed the audition," she said. "We really will have to find a way to see each other without having to pretend to read books."

"*I* read almost all of it," Derek said. He actually felt indignant about it now, and he could feel the poutiness creeping into his voice. "Am I the only one who even *tried*?"

She stood up from the chair and walked to where he was standing, at the threshold between the kitchen and living room. She put her hands on his shoulders and looked into his eyes with the solemnity of someone trying not to laugh.

"My friend," she said. "I think it's time someone told you: you are not as special as you think you are."

Was anyone, though? Could *she* be as special as he thought she was? He followed her gaze to their reflections in the dark television screen.

"Be that as it may!" he said. "I should get going."

"You *could* stay," she said. "I don't think either of us is in a fit state for, you know, *substantive engagement* right now, and I'm, as you know all too well, *slightly* attached, but, I don't know. It's a big bed."

Even after an oil tanker's worth of vodka, even in the comforting dim light of the apartment he'd dreamed about more than once, he knew better. He would go home, text her in the morning. It was an investment, his decency. It would accrue interest. He didn't understand anything about money.

"You've gotta get to sleep," he said. "I bet Kyla wakes up early."

"Ugh, she *better* not," Violet said. She went to the kitchen and filled a glass of water from the tap. "I'm locking my door."

She seemed to have already put her vague offer aside; it probably hadn't had the significance he'd given it. He probably *should* have just stayed. That would have been a normal, friendly thing to do. *Proof* that he didn't harbor some ulterior motive. What *year* was it that he was so concerned about propriety? If it had been the sixties, like it should have been, or even, hell, the *nineties* . . .

"Let's do something soon," he said. "Please?"

"For sure, for sure," she said. "Oh wait!"

She picked up a book off the coffee table. Morgan Calder. *Some Other Way of Living.*

"Tell me how it ends?" she said. "Please?"

He opened the book to the pensively half-smiling author photo on the jacket. The guy still had most of his hair, but at least he was old. In ten years, he'd be *really* old, and Derek would only be thirty-five.

"My expectations," he said, "are out of control."

"If you hate it . . ." she said. "Well, try not to hate it."

He paged through the book under streetlights on the way home. First paragraph: way too long. How many clauses did one man need? Last sentence: something about a Carolyn "emerging carelessly" from a car. Indeed. There was no inscription. No underlining. No marginal notes. It was petty, he knew—definitely not worthy of the midwestern rookie of the year—but it felt *so fucking good* to drop the book in the trash can in front of his building. He would buy her a new one if she asked for it back.

The Changed Party

I WAS EATING A PLUM OVER the sink when my eight-year-old daughter Amanda slipped into the kitchen and started picking through the trash. She pulled out some crumpled plastic and pieces of old food, examining each item carefully before setting it on the counter. My plum dripped dark red drops into a coffee cup filled with water as I struggled toward a casual intervention.

"What are you doing there, honey?" I said.

"Checking to see if I threw anything away by accident," Amanda said. She held up a yogurt carton and shook it deliberately over the counter, sending tiny purple splatters across the tile.

"Are you missing something?"

"I don't *know*, that's why I'm *looking*."

The logic was just short of airtight. Amanda had woken up in the middle of the night a few times in the past month, coming into our room to tell us she was worried she'd left something behind at her day camp or at a friend's house.

Lisa or I would walk her back to her room and go through her possessions, accounting for everything of value, but it didn't seem to settle her. This was an escalation.

"Honey, I think you need to stop now," I said. "There's nothing in there."

"You don't know," Amanda said.

"Trust me," I said. "I've been alive a lot longer than you and I've never thrown away anything by accident."

I threw my plum pit in the bin for emphasis and brushed the trash she'd put on the counter in too. Amanda watched accusingly and picked at the back of her scalp.

"Why don't you go find Patrick and I'll take you guys to the arcade?" I said. It was raining again and we'd already seen two loud, terrible movies.

"*Fine*," she said, and slumped out of the kitchen.

We'd been at my mother's beach house on the Jersey shore for three days, with four still to go. My wife Lisa and I were there with Amanda, plus our friend Mike and his wife Victoria and their son Patrick. (My mother was on a bus tour of the West with her no-longer-new husband.) Lisa and I had recently reunited after a six-month separation, and hosting our old friends was serving as a kind of official acknowledgment that we were recommitted to this thing. For a variety of reasons, that was only going medium-well.

Lisa was in Atlantic City with Victoria for the day. They had been very clear that Mike and I were to interrupt only in the case of life-threatening emergency. The men and women had been trading day shifts with the kids because we all agreed that a rainy day with all six of us in that house would end in at least one fatality. Mike and I had spent our day off watching insignificant sporting events in the cavernous, gaudily renovated bar in the middle of town. I'd stopped drinking, out of necessity, after my third beer, but Mike made sure to keep putting down enough for both of us.

Now he was in the Florida room, shirtless, drinking vodka out of a tall glass. His curly blond hair had recently crept up to the top of his forehead, and his face was significantly wider and redder than it had been when we met as freshmen at Northwestern. He was still, as my mother would say, *a nice-looking man*, as long as you didn't focus on his belly.

"Al Pacino is shit," he said, jerking his drink toward the TV. "*Godfather*, *Serpico*, sure. After that? Garbage."

"I'm going to take the kids to the arcade," I said.

"Didn't we take them yesterday?"

"Two days ago," I said.

He sank deeper into the couch. "They should use their imaginations. Do a play for us or something."

"I already told Amanda," I said. "You can stay here."

"Nope, nope." He hoisted himself to his feet. "Gotta support the team." He patted his pockets. "Wallet, phone. Good to go."

He pitched forward and caught himself, then snuck a glance at me to see if I'd noticed.

"Why don't you stay here?" I said.

"Gonna find that kid," he muttered, and walked toward the kitchen.

Amanda was sitting by the front door putting on her shoes.

"Patrick is being weird," she whispered.

"That's not nice," I said, though of course he *was* weird. Patrick was prone to alternating bouts of hyperactivity and glassy-eyed silence. He was a couple of years younger than Amanda, but they'd always gotten along all right before now. And—of course I couldn't say this—who was she, given our kitchen debacle, to talk?

"He keeps playing the same song over and over and he won't let me talk or anything when it's on," she said.

"What song?" I said.

"'Everybody Wants to Be a Cat.'"

"At least it's a good one," I said.

"It's okay," she said.

"You guys coming?" I called back into the house. Patrick and Mike shuffled slowly around the corner like they were expecting a Minotaur. Mike had put on a neon-orange polo shirt with a dark stain on the belly. He had a can of beer in his hand and another bulging from the pocket of his khaki shorts. Patrick's sneakers were untied and he was wearing a Spider-Man bathing suit and no shirt. They stared at me with the same half-lidded eyes, awaiting instruction.

"You really don't have to come," I said.

"Whaddya think, bud?" Mike said. "Watch the end of *Devil's Advocate* with Daddo? Blurred-out boobies?"

"Arcaaaaade," Patrick said, jogging in place.

"Right you are!" Mike said. "Onward, Christian monsters!"

I would have insisted we walk, since it was only ten blocks away, but since it was raining—always—we piled into the Outback. Mike fell into the passenger seat and put on the pink sunglasses he found in the cup holder.

"Seat belts!" he hollered, facing forward.

"Patrick needs a shirt," Amanda said.

"It's not the fucking yacht club," Mike said.

"Hey," I said.

"Gosh, I'm sorry, honey." He twisted around in his seat. "Uncle Mike didn't mean that. It's not the *stinkin'* yacht club, right? *We don't need no stinkin' yacht club*, right? No?"

"You need to pull it together," I said quietly when he'd turned back around.

He cracked open a beer.

"EVER-BODY! EVER-BODY!" screamed Patrick. "EVER-BODY WANTS TO BE A CAT!"

Mike turned up the volume on the radio until "Umbrella" blasted from the speakers for the thousandth time that summer. In the rearview mirror I saw Amanda with her face pressed against the window.

We pulled into the parking lot and ran through the rain and up the steps of the small boardwalk to the arcade. It was a buzzing, clanging place, with prize shelves piled with boxed blenders and stuffed animals. I'd loved arcades and all manner of deafening silliness when I was a kid, but now it gave me an instant headache. I fed a five-dollar bill into a change machine—the saddest action of fatherhood?—and the quarters crashed into the metal dispenser. I scooped them up and dropped them into Amanda's clear-plastic ticket bucket.

"Don't use these up too fast," I said.

"I just want tickets," Amanda said. She hadn't cashed in the ones she'd earned on Monday, and she still had reams left over from last summer as well. She wouldn't tell me what she was saving them for. It wasn't clear that she knew.

"Do you need money?" I said to Mike. I asked nicely. Mike never had cash when we went places but he always paid me back. He worked for an investment firm and made more money than Lisa and me combined—he and Victoria had a house in Newton that I would have envied if I cared about things like that.

"Nah, Patrick doesn't want to play any games," he said. "Do you, Patrick?"

This set off a high-pitched whine.

"Use your words," Mike said.

"*Games*," said Patrick.

I put another five bucks in the machine.

"Don't mess with him, Mike," I said.

Mike scooped a handful of quarters from the dispenser. "I'm gonna go play the gator whack," he said to Patrick. "You can come, or you can stay here by the quarter machine being an asshole."

Mike started walking and Patrick clung to his shirt, letting himself be dragged off to a corner of the arcade. I looked around for Amanda and saw her by a big machine with a multicolored light spinning around inside it.

"What are you playing, honey?" I said.

"If you stop the light in the right place you get a thousand tickets," Amanda said. "And if you get it close you still get some tickets for trying."

"Is it fun?" I said.

"Yeah," she said without enthusiasm. Amanda was such a serious kid, incredibly smart for her age, and lacking any useful outlet for her grimness. So far, she liked scary movies and building things; the happiest I'd ever seen her was when she helped construct a haunted house with her friends and then played a screaming, bloody murder victim in it. What would happen to her in her life? Could her brilliance outrun her anxiety? I spent a lot of time worrying about it.

I watched her play the game. It was hypnotic, and I found myself willing the stupid light to stop in the right place for her. It wasn't happening. I got a text from Lisa: "AC's kind of a drag, we'll be home in an hour." I was glad they were coming back but I worried about the scene that would ensue when Vic saw how drunk Mike was.

I found him with Patrick at the Skee-Ball machines. Mike was rolling the wooden balls too hard, beer in hand, while Patrick clambered up and down the machine next to his.

"Offa there, Pat," Mike said.

"Throw it to me, Dad!" Patrick said. He was perched at the top hole of his Skee-Ball machine, clinging to the protective netting. Mike ignored him.

"So Lisa says they're bailing on AC," I said. "They're on their way back now."

"Guess we should cancel the strippers," Mike said.

"Let's sober up," I said. "I don't want to go through the Eugene O'Neill routine with you and Vic."

Mike took off his sunglasses. "Old buddy, with all due respect, I can handle my wife."

"Great," I said. "That's great."

"Dad, we need more balls!" Patrick shouted.

"Let's go get a prize, Pat," Mike said.

"We didn't get enough tickets," Patrick said, but he followed him to the counter. I got Amanda and stood with her outside under the awning, watching the rain. Mike would probably apologize when he was sober, but I wasn't sure what good it would do. Time had run out on this thing we'd had, probably. I heard him yelling inside.

"Look, man, he wants the Ninja Turtle. The thing's been on your shelf since 1989. I'll give you twenty bucks. Tell your manager I wouldn't take no for an answer. Because I fucking won't."

"Stay here," I said to Amanda. I went back into the arcade and saw that Mike was behind the counter, with the wispy-bearded employee blocking him from escaping with the toy.

"I don't want there to be an incident," the kid said.

"That's on you, bud," Mike said. "I'm trying to fucking *pay* for it."

"That's a ten-thousand-ticket prize," the kid said. "It takes a shit-ton more than twenty bucks to win that many tickets."

I felt a surge of solidarity with Mike—even twenty bucks was an absurd price for this junk—but also, he was being an idiot.

"Let's go, Mike," I said. "He's got to follow the rules. We'll pick up some stuff for the kids in town."

Mike met my eyes and I saw a flicker of humanity— King Kong deciding not to throw Fay Wray off the Empire State Building. He reached below the counter, snatched a plastic basket of bouncy balls, and chucked a fistful of them into the arcade, where they careened off of the machines and rolled crazily across the floor.

"Good customer service here," Mike said. "Call me if you ever need a job." He dropped the Ninja Turtle on the floor and hoisted himself clumsily over the counter.

"Don't you ever come back in here," the kid said to Mike's back.

"Hey, I'm sorry about all this," I said to the kid, taking out my wallet.

"You too," he said. "You should know better than to let people like that into a place full of kids."

I mean, he was right.

Lisa and I had been together, happily unmarried, for five years when we decided to try to have a kid. We had a big family wedding at a hotel down the street from the beach house, soon after which Lisa got pregnant and had Amanda. (Best not to count the months on that one, actually.) These were good years. I was a senior editor at a news aggregator during a brief window of profitability, a job I didn't have to care too much about. Lisa was able to quit her EPA job to stay home with Amanda for the first couple of years and get by with some consulting on the side. When she went back to work directing an environmental nonprofit, Amanda was in preschool, and I was able to fix my schedule around picking her up and watching her in the afternoons.

One night, Lisa came home from a fund-raising trip asking for an open marriage. When I pressed her on the reason, she told me, after a few deflections, that she'd been sleeping with her friend Tim, with whom she'd gone to Dartmouth, and felt terrible about it. She cried, I cried. She agreed to break it off, then didn't. The other guy made his case for true love, reminded her that life was short—all that nineteenth-century shit. (He was an assistant professor of literature at Amherst, but his guy was Wallace Stevens. Dignity isn't transmitted via dissertation.) My reliably cynical wife, with a degree in art history and a master's in water engineering, bought it.

On a Sunday afternoon in March, she drove from our apartment in Boston out to Western Massachusetts, taking her clothes, books, and some random kitchen supplies. It was an indefinite experiment. She'd commute or work from wherever they were living, or something—for all I knew, Vronsky was promising to take care of her with his trust fund. We agreed that Amanda would visit her on the weekends and during school vacations. She had just turned seven, and we agreed to spin the separation as a work-related necessity until we figured out something better.

At the time, I resented the fact that Amanda's upkeep stopped me from drinking myself sick and calling every former classmate and coworker I'd ever wanted to sleep with, but in retrospect that was for the best. I had some weekend adventures (piano bar to hotel bar to hotel *room*) and some long nights with the HBO roster. But as terrible as I felt—and, according to my friends, I was nearly catatonic for significant stretches during this period—I was pretty sure it wouldn't be how things ended with Lisa. It was so far from the way she'd handled her life in all of the preceding years that I couldn't imagine it was permanent. (She also, according to both mother and daughter, hadn't introduced her new friend to Amanda, which must have been logistically difficult.) Another obvious possibility—that she was a fundamentally different person from the one I'd always thought her to be—was so painful that I tried not to let myself entertain it too often.

In any case, after months of minimal communication (necessary kid stuff only), I brought Amanda home from day camp and found Lisa sitting on the couch, wearing the flower-specked sundress I'd bought her for her birthday the year before. She cried, I cried; she begged forgiveness, I held out. Tim was an egomaniac, she said. He'd expected her to keep house for him while he worked on his book and schmoozed for tenure—Shirley Jackson all over again. She missed me (well, compared to that guy, sure), missed Amanda (obviously), hated Amherst (tell it to Emily Dickinson).

That first night she stayed home while I went out for a drink with Mike. Sure, he agreed, it was shitty, but if I still loved her, I had to forgive her and try to fix things. Because wasn't this what I'd said I wanted? And, more importantly, wasn't it the best thing for Amanda? Some version of this thought emerged as the consensus among my friends, family, fellow content aggregators. Mike's wife Victoria was a notable exception. She cited "trust." But see, I said, I wouldn't ever trust *anyone* again, so if you looked at it that way, she was only as untrustworthy as everyone else! Vic was not convinced.

Lisa slept in the guest room while we went to twice-weekly therapy sessions, during which she apologized and heaped scorn on the erstwhile emperor of ice cream. Why, if he was so awful, did she destroy her life to be with him? Well, she'd wanted to be in love with a new person. She knew now that she hadn't been. He talked a big game but at the end of the day he was a selfish partner and a derivative scholar. I understood this on an intellectual level, but I couldn't bring myself to empathize. One night in October, she crept back into our room and we had the kind of terrifying sex that can only be had by an emotionally drained, long-separated couple trying to prove something complicated. We stopped seeing the therapist and, at least for a couple of months, fucked our way to some kind of détente.

Back at the house I coaxed Mike into taking a shower and put *Beetlejuice* on for the kids for what must have been the tenth time. I deserved a beer, and my head was pounding, but I didn't want to temper my self-righteousness. I opened the latest book about how badly we'd fucked up Iraq and watched Alec Baldwin and Geena Davis out of the corner of my eye.

Mike came in wearing boxers, toweling his hair. "Word from the girls?"

"No," I said.

"Still pissed at me, got it." He walked into the kitchen and opened the refrigerator. I tried to focus on my book, the movie, anything but Mike's intake. I was resentful about having to even think the word "intake." He came back in with a drink and sat down next to me, still wearing nothing but his boxers.

"Winona Ryder, goin' inside her," he said gravely.

Patrick crawled up onto the couch and squeezed in be-tween us. When our wives came in, Mike was nearly done with his second drink.

"Isn't *this* cozy," said Lisa. "Where's Amanda?"

I looked to the floor where she'd been sitting.

"Not here?" I said. I really was puzzled, but I know it came out glib.

"Amanda!" Lisa called, moving into the house. Victo-ria gave Mike and me a glance and headed off down the hallway to the bedrooms. I watched the movie for a couple more minutes, but when Lisa didn't come back I got up to find her. I walked through the Florida room and saw them on the back porch. Amanda was sitting behind a pile of trash—not just kitchen stuff but bloody tissues and vacuum cleaner dirt and even a couple of diapers (from *where?*), with the tall kitchen bin and the wicker trash baskets from the house scattered around her. I gave myself a three count before sliding back the glass door.

"Yes, you *will* get sick playing in the trash," Lisa was saying. "When things rot, they decompose, and they grow mold. And if you touch them, and you touch your face, even if you don't mean to, you get very, very sick."

"I'm not *playing*," Amanda said.

"Honey, I told you to stop with this," I said.

Lisa pivoted, shifting her anger toward me like a heavy suitcase.

"She was going through the garbage in the kitchen ear-lier," I said.

"It would have been *awesome* if you had told me that, dude," she said.

"Amanda, go inside," I said. "Wash your hands and go watch the movie with Patrick."

She opened her mouth to protest, but then thought better of it and went.

"I am *not* trying to be a hard-ass," Lisa said. "But seriously."

"I've been babysitting Mike and the kids all afternoon," I said. "It's been, you know, raining and about to rain."

I didn't even get a raised eyebrow.

"*I* came home to Amanda going through used tampons."

"I don't know how it happened!" I yelled. "I *said* I was sorry, right?"

She exhaled slowly.

"I really hope this doesn't become more of a thing," she said in a smaller voice. "It's so hard to figure out where *your* head's at, and if *she's* a mess . . ."

"We'll do what we have to do," I said. "We'll sort it out."

"Is Michael drunk?"

"I mean, he's drinking."

"Victoria is going to kill him," Lisa said. "I really can't go through the *Long Day's Journey* routine right now."

At least our points of reference were still aligned. We bent down and started putting the trash in the big kitchen bag. As a gesture of solidarity, you couldn't ask for much better.

"What should we do tonight?" I said.

"I was thinking four-way," Lisa said.

"That tank top on Vic?" I said.

"Yeah?" Lisa said. "You like that?"

"In a pinch, sure."

"A pinch," Lisa said. "Christ."

I took the bulging garbage bag out to the curb and went to get another one. Victoria had taken my seat on the couch with Mike and Patrick. She looked at me with a warning: *Don't destroy this peace, ephemeral as it may be. Believe me*, I tried to convey back telepathically, *it's the furthest thing from my mind.*

After a while, I got up and made spaghetti. Patrick dropped all of his silverware on the floor. Mike ostentatiously drank water at dinner, but he was glazed over, and I figured he was sneaking vodka. The rain let up and we decided, why the hell not, to walk for ice cream. Mike and Lisa walked ahead with the kids while Victoria and I hung back.

Victoria had cut her hair short and I wasn't sure yet how I felt about it. She had large, fabulously expressive features, and her eyes and nose now seemed almost abandoned without her long hair to frame them. Ahead of us, I saw Lisa with her head inclined toward Mike while he made extravagant arm gestures. Watching them walk together, I remembered how much Lisa had actually liked him, before everyone had to take sides.

"I hope Patrick normalizes," Victoria was saying. "It'll be hard for him. Otherwise."

"I was pretty hyper when I was that age," I said. "He's a good kid, though. That's the important thing. Probably."

"Are you worried about Amanda?"

"I suppose I'm *concerned*," I said. "Do you think I should worry?"

"I just know it's hard to see your kid unhappy," she said.

"It's our responsibility to provide the *opportunities* for happiness, but we can't *make* them be happy."

"There's therapy," I said. "Drugs."

"You've got to be careful with that, though," she said. "Once you start trying things—the drugs, I mean—you're kind of obliged to see it through. It can get really hairy. I mean, whatever, you know I've been medicated since I was sixteen, I don't know why I'm being cagey." She took off her glasses and pressed her palms into her eyes. "Anyway. Lisa seems better. Right? I'm pretty impressed slash shocked by where you guys are at."

"We put on a good show," I said.

"I might murder Michael," she said. "But I think we'll probably stay together until then."

Why? was my obvious follow-up question. But Patrick came running toward us, crying that it was too far for him to walk. Amanda was off by herself, staring at the sidewalk. I left Victoria to deal with Patrick and caught up with Lisa and Mike.

"Do you ever feel this way, Gary?" Lisa said. "Mike was talking about how sometimes he'll read a client summary that he wrote years before and not recognize it at all."

"I mean, I'll remember the *act* of writing it," Mike said. "But when I look at it, I can't imagine being as articulate as I apparently *was*. It's kind of interesting."

I did not weigh in on the likelihood of alcohol-induced brain damage.

"When I was moving stuff a little while ago, I found an old notebook from college," Lisa said, quickly moving ahead before mentioning *why* she had been moving her stuff. "It was full of all this detailed analysis of Renaissance sculptures. And they weren't just notes copied from the board. They were my *thoughts* on these things. And now it's all just *gone*. If you put a gun to my head I wouldn't be able to tell you about . . . I don't even know what. I just looked at it and I still don't remember the names. Boccio? Is that one?"

"It's in there somewhere," I said. I hoped it was, at least.

The ice-cream place came into view, the line of families and dogs stretching around the block.

"C'mon, guys," I called back to the kids, trying to wrangle them before the line got longer.

"I've got to find somewhere to piss," Mike said. "I'll meet you guys there in a sec."

"Why don't you just wait with us?" Lisa said. "We were having a good talk."

"Sorry, dear, I can't be pissing my pants in front of all these respectable folks."

"Michael, do not go have a drink," Victoria said.

"I told you what I'm going to do," Mike said.

"Then take Patrick with you," Victoria said. "He needs to go, too."

"*Ice* cream," Patrick said.

"Go with your father," Victoria said. "We'll be in line when you get back."

"He doesn't want to go, Vic," Mike said. "I'm not gonna drag him screaming into the bathroom with me."

"You are an incredibly selfish person," Victoria said. "That's the last thing I'm going to say."

"I doubt that," Mike said. He stalked off in the direction we'd come from.

"*Go*," Lisa stage-whispered to me. I jogged half a block to catch up with him, saw him sip from a battered Poland Spring bottle and grimace.

"Cavalry's here," he said. "I was worried I'd be trusted on my own for one fucking second."

He offered me the water bottle, and, forgive me, I took a small, bitter sip. We were in front of Tom's, the last dive bar left in town. (It was torn down a couple of years later, along with everything else on the block, to make room for more condos.)

"You know I don't want to babysit you," I said.

"Seriously," Mike said. "You want to be able to talk to a person. And all you get is this *shit*."

He looked so bereft in that moment that I put my hand on his shoulder, a prelude to a hug, I thought, or at least a sympathetic gripping. But he pulled away from me. He looked me right in the eyes and raised the half-full water bottle of vodka to his mouth, sucking hard on the white spigot and swallowing theatrically. The plastic crumpled loudly in his hand as his face grew red and his eyes watered.

"Like a house on *fi-yah*," he said when he had finished it.

"Let me take you home," I said. "Before you fall over."

"Naw, gonna check this place out," he said. He went in and I stood outside, staring at the door. I thought he might come back out, or get shoved out like a saloon cowboy, but he didn't. I walked back to the ice-cream line.

"Where's Michael?" Victoria said.

"In the bar," I said. I hated to see her shudder, but I was also relieved. I was done taking responsibility.

On our way back to the house, Victoria stepped into Tom's but Mike wasn't there anymore; she tried his cell phone and got nothing. When we got back to the house, he wasn't passed out on the couch, as I'd stupidly hoped he might be. We waited an hour and Victoria drove out to check the other bars on the island. She phoned me from the last place: Should she call the police? It had only been a couple of hours, I told her. If he wanted to be out without answering his phone, he was allowed. She came back and the three of us put the kids to bed. We turned on the TV and watched an awful show about a sex-murderer. By the time the news came on, Victoria was pacing the room.

"Look, this isn't the first time he's done this," Lisa said.

"I have a really bad feeling," Victoria said. "I just have this feeling that he really doesn't want to come back."

"He seemed fine when we were walking," Lisa said. "He was being very sweet, actually."

"That's what he does," Victoria said. "He makes you think everything's okay just so he can go and destroy it."

"I don't think it's intentional," I said.

"Yeah, well, the result is the same," Victoria said.

Lisa and I went to our room under the pretext of getting ready for bed.

"Do you think he's all right?" Lisa said. "Should we go look for him?"

"He knows where the house is," I said. "He'll come back if he wants to."

"Why are you being like that?"

"Because I'm tired," I said. I made sure to keep my voice even. "*You* go if you're worried. Hey, bring the kids."

"You're pissed at *me*?"

"Not particularly," I said.

"Right, so, in short, yes," she said. "I know I've said it a hundred times, but you can't be mad at me forever. That's not going to work."

I sat down next to her on the bed.

"'Indefinitely' isn't a great time frame, either," she said. "Hey. Look at me."

I did. Her head was cocked and I knew she was on the verge of breaking out a sympathetic smile.

"It's just me," she said.

"How do you think you've changed since we got back together?" I said.

She canceled the smile and sat up straight.

"You know how much more I appreciate what we have now. And that I know now what I *don't* want, and how important that's been for me." It was a speech she'd given before.

"Right, but how are *you* different? You *see* things differently, I get that, but what about *you*? *You* you."

"What do you want?" she said. "'I've gained ten pounds'? I wasn't perfect before but I don't think I'm worse now."

"So you're saying it's me," I said.

"I don't know what the 'it' in that sentence refers to."

She'd been deposed many times, most recently in a dispute between her group and the West Virginia Department of Environmental Protection over acceptable level of bacterial pathogens in groundwater systems. I had a dismal record in our arguments.

"The changed party," I said. "That's the 'it.' Maybe I've changed."

"You seem the same to me," she said.

I stood up and let my thoughts settle.

"I'm not being very articulate," I said. "I'm fine, I guess. Fine enough."

"Are you?" Lisa said. I could tell she actually cared, and I wanted to know the answer, too.

"I'm going to check on Amanda and see what Victoria's story is," I said. I closed the door behind me before she could respond.

When I cracked open the door to the kids' room, two sets of eyes stared back at me from the bottom bunk. Night creatures.

"We can't sleep," Patrick said.

"Where's Uncle Mike?" said Amanda.

"He's taking a walk," I said. "Honey, get in your own bed."

She clambered up to the top bunk and I tucked her in.

"Patrick and I were trying to figure out what I threw away," Amanda said.

"You need to stop with this," I said.

"I need to look in that barrel at the arcade," she said. "I know that's where it is."

"Where what is?"

"Something important," she said.

I remembered that we weren't allowed back in that

arcade. It was a small mercy. "Go to sleep. Maybe Mom can take you to check in the morning."

Patrick whimpered in the bottom bunk. I put his blanket over him and he quieted down. In the living room, Victoria was in the armchair, texting ferociously.

"My sister thinks I should call the police if I think he's a danger to himself or others," she said.

She put down her phone and sank deeper into the chair.

"Vic, you deserve better than this," I said. "We all do."

"It's just exhausting," she said. "Why is it so impossible to just relax and be a person?"

It still seemed to me, then, that it was wrong to relax, that it was better to fight against Mike's drinking and Lisa's inconstancy and Amanda's whatever-it-was than to accept things for what they were. I'd already tried complacency with Lisa, I thought, and learned that it bred disaster. But this was before I understood that going through these problems again and again—and we would, for a few more years to come, be in a similar place, attempting to understand and control our children, failing to tame our wayward partners—was the worst kind of complacency, a refusal to take responsibility for our own happiness. It took me a long time.

Victoria got up from the chair and sat down on the couch next to me. I rubbed her back and mouthed empty clichés as she sat hunched over and watched *Big* on TV through her fingers. Eventually she lay down with her head in my lap and fell asleep almost immediately. I felt a flood of protectiveness toward her, and some concomitant, uncalculated desire. I registered the shifts Victoria made as she slept, felt the wistful texture of her fluff of hair. It scared me.

I put a blanket over her and gently shifted her head from my lap onto the couch cushion. She made an unconscious murmur of protest and settled back into sleep. I sat down to read in the armchair across the room, but mostly just watched Vic's breath rise and fall. When I got to the point where I was hallucinating extra presences in the room from exhaustion, I went back into our room to lay awake next to Lisa.

Mike did come home, close to dawn. He and Vic had a fight that left a picture frame broken and the kids in tears. When I stepped out of our room he went out the front door and took off in his car. He got arrested outside Pittsburgh after crashing through a toll lane barrier with a .21 BAC. Victoria rented a car and drove up there to deal with him, so Lisa and I watched Patrick for the rest of the week. That old Davy Crockett song became his tune of choice (he had a CD of Disney classics stashed away somewhere), and when I think about those days, I hear "killed him a bear, when he was only three" in that goofball old-timey voice.

Patrick, who is growing into a smart, kind man, says he doesn't remember that. He remembers burying Amanda up to her neck in sand on the beach after the rain finally let up for good. That day is vivid in my mind, too. Amanda begged to stay there, stuck like that, even when the wind picked up and Lisa made the call that it was time to head home. Patrick got frustrated and started digging up the sand around her neck, flinging it into her eyes and hair.

Over Amanda's screams, I told him to cut it out. We packed up all of our things, making a big singsong show of leaving without her, and then, when she made no attempt at escape, we started trudging up toward the dunes to the street.

"Goodbye!" she called to our backs. "I love you! Visit soon!"

Attention

began in the garden of the house in Surrey, crunching on chips and watching her brother swing on a tattered karate belt from the crotch of a low tree. The belt broke, or the branch, she wasn't sure, and he slammed to the ground on his back. She remembered the panic in his eyes and his silence before the air came back into his lungs. She ran inside as he began to howl, certain she was witnessing death, even if she didn't have the name for it. She was excited, but mostly terrified by this revelation of the world's dark secret. Her brother was fine. Philip, later, could not pick out that particular minor injury from a childhood rife with them. But it stuck with her. In her imagined memory of it, there was a soft voice in her head saying, *I am three now and I can think now, I am in the sun and I am alive*, and then sudden movement and the crash, the gasping and screaming, and a return to blind instinct, further consciousness delayed until a more agreeable time.

———

She remembered herself as happy enough in those early years of patchy self-awareness, but in pictures and home movies (which she was glad she'd watched enough times to memorize before the obsolescence of the technology on which they were captured made them impossible to revisit), she looked worried, or more often simply confused by what was going on around her. She'd been an *easy child* in most ways, she'd been told, but when she thought about it now, she was angry that she'd been *allowed* to be easy, that she hadn't been encouraged to put up more of a fight against complacency or timidity or whatever it was that had kept her from experiencing more of the highs and lows that were presumably the hallmarks of most childhoods.

She'd had more than her share of *disasters*—before she turned five, Cassie had smashed her head open on a cabinet door, consumed a bottle of cough medicine, fallen in the deep end of a pool—but these were matters of distraction, misunderstanding. Accidents. In the case of the near-drowning, she remembered thinking, as she sank deeper below the water, *Oh, this again.* She could see the tiles at the bottom glistening distractedly before her father fished her out.

It wasn't that she hadn't wanted to be noticed. Someone—like, a therapist, say, if she allowed herself to afford one—might suggest that she'd had a sublimated desire to be fussed over. But it didn't feel that way. She was more attached to her father than her mother, even though, or because, like most fathers, hers was much less frequently available than she would have liked. Philip more obviously took after their mother. They were both dark-haired and voluble, chattering constantly about whatever came into their heads. Cassie wasn't *silent*, but she often wasn't sure what she was supposed to say, and thus waited for cues, sometimes long past the point at which they would have arrived, had they been coming. Philip never seemed to have this problem, and she understood on some level that the *volume* of words he produced was in part what kept any of them in particular from taking on an outsized importance to him. Talking was a form of thinking for him, whereas for her, the activities were related but far from intertwined. Her thoughts more often than not canceled each other out with their contradictions, making it difficult to know what should actually be spoken out loud. And then when she did speak she often found herself saying the opposite of what she'd meant, or at best some muddled approximation of it, and then spent the next minutes or hours reproaching herself for not being more capable of clear expression. Philip and her parents brought it to her attention that she had developed the wisp of an English accent, which no one else in the family had, and she was both proud and self-conscious about this. It was one of many things about which she would feel both proud and self-conscious. When they moved back to "the States," to Connecticut when she was ten, her accent melted in the summer heat and she sounded like she could be from anywhere.

———

Her father was not a quiet person, but he did not speak freely like her mother did. He spoke either quite seriously or in a silly voice, and he repeated things often. He had catchphrases, many of which, she would learn later, were from the television shows and movies of his youth. One that she liked to join in on was "You are a P-I-G pig!" delivered in something suggesting a southern accent. She liked repetition. She liked to watch the same videos again and again until she had memorized them and could mouth along with what the characters on the screen were saying. Then she could reenact her favorite scenes quietly to herself while she lay in bed trying to fall asleep. Sometimes she would sleep in Philip's room, in the bunk bed, and he would tell her stories, often featuring the characters she liked best from her videos. She enjoyed his attention, and so she tried not to complain too much when the actions of the characters deviated from what they'd actually done in the real version. She told herself that Philip's stories (not in these words exactly at the time) would have no bearing on the canon whose truth she could always return to later.

What she loved most of all was when her father told her and Philip stories before bed. Her father was not, she learned as she grew older, a naturally creative person, which made his modest efforts more impressive in retrospect. (Their mother, the more serious reader, served as the amanuensis for their diaries when it was her turn to put them to bed—if they'd been trying to raise writers, which they hadn't been, consciously, they would have been hard-pressed to come up with a better plan.) Her father would tell stories about Prince Philip and Princess Cassandra and their court, which was made up of their real-life friends and family members. The content of the stories consisted almost entirely of long lists of names, and if any was left off, Cassie made sure to inquire after them, for fear that someone had died or been banished. But they were all present, all fine. Philip would occasionally betray an impatience to get to the narrative portion of the story, which usually consisted of a fairly rote dragon slaying or the rescuing of the princess from a vague but diabolical kidnapper. Their father was, she could see now, helped along greatly by his children's pestering desire for more information, forcing him to provide details he hadn't thought necessary. Where did the dragon *come* from? Well . . . the lake. Was it a deep lake? Yes. How deep? Four thousand feet. Whoa, that's *really* deep. Are there *other* dragons down there? . . . No, just the one. The other ones died? . . . No. They moved away. Like we moved to England. But there was one that didn't want to move. And that's why he kidnapped the princess. *Ohhhh.*

It was good for their imaginations to have a father with a relative dearth of one. Cassie asked him later, after she started writing plays, whether he'd found it stressful, as a structural engineer by trade, to come up with stories to tell them. "Not really," he said. "You seemed pretty happy with whatever I said."

———

She worked in an office now, as her father had, to pay her rent, and she went over the plots of movies she'd seen to make the minutes go by.

She was thirty-two, the age at which other peoples' tattoos begin to feel like personal affronts. Jaunty skeleton, fake suture, wilted rose: stop. She had a single word of text branded below the knob of her left ankle. On the rare occasions when people noticed it, they were mildly amused. Some people knew her for years before they discovered it; others never did. It was what she aspired to on many fronts—the slow reveal of character, the possession of a personhood that could not be grasped whole without effort expended.

She'd learned that the key to email at work was to respond quickly, even if you didn't have anything coherent or helpful to say. "Thanks for this!" was a good way to start. Then: "Let me check up on that and follow up with you soon." Ideally, this was where the exchange ended, but all too often the correspondent took that burst of vague professionalism as a license to continue pestering her. She waited for texts from her brother—he currently reported on science from Mexico City—and for the moment between 5:00 and 5:30 when it would be appropriate for her to leave the office, depending on what time she'd managed to arrive.

After the workday, she hoped to produce some writing, maybe have dinner or watch a movie with the new maybe-boyfriend. Friendship, she was deciding, was a childish conceit, an affectation possessed by people who imagined that the conditions of their lives circa age eighteen would remain basically the same in perpetuity. She'd previously been a fan of this conceit—she just wished she hadn't seen through it.

She lamented the fact that her new coworkers only saw her shadow self, quiet and obliging and maybe a little bit lazy. Ruefully funny on occasion, sure, but always within the bounds of office decorum. Her other self was for her family and the Internet, and maybe Leonard, if he stuck around.

Anyway, she was pretty sure her coworkers were plotting against her. Office life made her paranoid—she *was* being *watched*, after all—but things had gotten worse lately. In the mornings, Eleanor, her boss, a beautiful, curt, fundamentally decent woman of sixty, brushed past her door without a word. Her hallmate, the last remaining communications associate still based in the United States, seemed to have her door closed at all hours of the day. Around the corner, Douglas, whose most valued trait was the presence of a faithfully forbearing Saint Bernard curled heavily in his office's Ikea chair, gave her only monosyllables when she stopped by, his eyes fixed on his massive monitor. The only person who responded normally to her was Greta, the department assistant, who, Cassie feared, was herself at risk of losing her job for her laissez-faire attitude toward task fulfillment and flagrant violations of the office dress code. Though Cassie still didn't consider this job her "real life," she also preferred not to be fired from it. She knew that she would start crying immediately if it was so much as suggested that there had been a lapse in her work, even if it was, to be honest, mostly lapses at this point. She did not want them to see her cry. She thought that Eleanor might be able to maintain a vaguely empathetic expression on her face for the minutes it would take to dismiss her, though she knew that, inside, she would be disgusted.

In these caverns of anxiety, Cassie rarely spent much time speculating about what she would be fired *for*, exactly. It simply seemed inevitable. She took excessively long lunch breaks, sometimes pretending she was meeting with fake people about matters pertaining to the law school alumni magazine, the rewriting and fact-checking of whose articles was theoretically her day's occupation. She wandered the halls of the law school, sometimes watching a few silent minutes of a lecture in progress before accidentally catching the eye of a student or professor. Mostly, of course, she responded to personal emails or browsed the Internet trying to find a more interesting job. But surely this was how most people spent their workdays?

The alternative to imminent dismissal—that her colleagues liked her fine, or at least as much as was necessary to not bother going through the arduous process of removing her—seemed fantastically optimistic. She was certain that *something* was being planned, something to which she was not privy. It seemed unlikely that, when they met behind closed doors without her, they were planning her a surprise birthday party. Her birthday had passed, unacknowledged, four months ago.

Greta, the assistant, appeared now in her doorway. She was a slightly implausible combination of certitude and naïveté, the exact admixture of which was only possible between the ages of twenty-two and twenty-four.

"Hey, do you have, like, that *document* that we're supposed to fill out?" she said. "I think it was for *health* insurance maybe?"

"Yeah, I can forward it to you," Cassie said.

"Okay, cool," Greta said. "But also, maybe, when you have time, could you, like, *explain* it to me? Like, just which one I should *do*, I guess?"

"You should do the cheaper one," Cassie said. "Unless you have some complicated medical issues that need attention."

Greta's eyes rose toward the ceiling, reviewing, presumably, her short medical history. They nearly reached her low-hanging blond bangs. She was wearing a purple jumpsuit that bagged around her torso like a full-body diaper, yet somehow looked extremely stylish on her.

"I don't . . . *think* I do?" she said. "I mean, I have pretty bad allergies and need to, like, get checked out for some stuff. But hopefully it won't be, you know, *complicated*."

"Do the cheaper one," Cassie said. "You'll be fine."

Greta nodded, hesitated.

"When you were my age, did you even, like, *have* health insurance? Wasn't it like a million dollars?"

Cassie grappled internally with the simplest way to explain an aspect of very recent history. How old did Greta think she was?

"When I was your age, I had a decent job, so I had good insurance. But a couple of years later I didn't, and I got through it. I got lucky. I got some basic stuff through Planned Parenthood and didn't really go to the doctor unless I had to. It was shitty, but, you know, I figured it out."

Greta ventured a small, victorious smile.

"So . . . it's *possible*—I'm not saying *good*, just *possible*—that it wouldn't be, like, the end of the world if the healthcare thing ends up getting killed."

Where did one begin? Where could one possibly end? She didn't blame the kid for the world's evil.

"It . . . it just isn't right," Cassie said. "We're young—or *you* are—and if you feel weird it's probably not going to turn out to be cancer. And if, God forbid, it is, your young body will fight it with your child blood. But if it's a thirty-five-year-old mom with two kids, and it's cancer, she's *fucked*, right? And if she dies, that's another generation fucked over, at least. If *you* die, no offense, your parents will be really sad, and your friends will, like, read poems off their phones at your funeral. *I'll* be really sad, obviously, because you're great. But it won't be a case study in the evils of late capitalism."

Greta shifted her weight, studied Cassie's messy desk thoughtfully.

"So . . . I *really* don't want to get cancer. If I *don't* want to get cancer, I should maybe just get the expensive plan?"

"Sure," Cassandra said. "Yes."

On the train home, she read a French graphic memoir about a miserable childhood. Hers had only been lonely because of her own choices, she thought. She had been loved as much as one could expect to be loved. She spent a lot of time thinking about it, all the little things that had happened. The captured newts, accidentally suffocated in Tupperware; the plastic bracelet, intentionally stolen from a comrade. The hours spent in bodies of water with Philip, their circular, deepening speculations about the nature of the world, the lies their parents told them, the existence of ghosts. Once, she had awoken to the bedsheets floating above her body. Once, they had stayed up all night wandering the halls of a purportedly haunted hotel and found nothing.

Her tendency toward disaster had continued into her late childhood, that is, until she was almost thirty. The disasters were still, she reckoned, accidents of carelessness. Being drunk increased the chances of a mistake. Being high gave her the elusive sense that all choices were not her own, that she was guided by some unyielding force of the universe. After a decade of the enforced stupidity of substances, sobriety felt like a magic trick. What, you got smarter by *not* doing things? She was careful with herself now, overly attentive to what went on around her. She didn't feel fragile, exactly. It was something like: she understood that the things of the world had weight and force, and that she did, too, and that, in combination, this could pose problems. She also sensed that the significant disasters of life—illness, marriage, children—might approach her less forthrightly than, say, a friend offering her some really excellent cocaine. She thought there was a chance that if she learned to recognize these small steps into the abyss, she might avoid, or at least postpone, the big ones.

At home, she poured herself a glass of orange juice and seltzer and drank it in front of her laptop, clicking between Word documents and the news. The world had been captured by the very stupid and evil—this was what Philip texted to tell her now most of the time, but she didn't mind it as much, coming from him. They were doomed and it mostly wasn't their fault. They'd been kind and artistic, and if they hadn't done as much as they should have for others, they at least hadn't actively made the world worse. They should have done more to stop their parents' participation in rapacious capitalism, but that was hard. Even

Marx took money from his parents, probably. Now that the world was over they were all donating money, chanting in public, crying on the phone.

No, she wasn't so cynical. She thought there was a chance that things could be made right eventually. She just couldn't imagine when that would be.

She wondered if her recent preoccupation with her childhood was a sign that things really were coming to an end, that it was her animal body's way of telling her that the only thing left to do was remember, because there would be no future for her or her friends. But then, so many people she knew were pregnant. Soon the office would be empty with maternity, and she, empty, filled to the brim with responsibility. The world was never just one thing.

When she and Philip were nine and seven, they'd produced a book together, him taking charge of the writing, she the illustrations. It was the story of a relationship, from a couple's first meeting through marriage, childbirth, parenting, and old age. She remembered wanting it to end with the pair's death—their great-grandmother had recently died, it was all she could think about—and Philip refusing. He had softer edges than she did. He was more generous, less outwardly afraid of things, though maybe it was because he refused to countenance them. She had drawn, on the back cover of their stapled production, two bloody corpses lying next to each other in the road. She could still picture the crude snuff illustration now, with her child scrawl underneath it: "THER DED." Philip had not been amused. At some point their mother framed the thing, so all you could see was the front cover, a cheerful, if distinctly motor-skill-challenged catalogue of the characters that would appear in the forthcoming pages. But Cassie knew what was on the other side.

Leonard, the man she was dating, did not seem likely to understand or transform her, but his presence made her feel a little better about the world, or slightly less vulnerable, at least, to falling off its edge. He was an account manager for a financial services company, which she found terrifying at first, but he seemed to genuinely not care very much about it. He did care seriously and with a relative lack of pretension about a number of things—skiing, watches, wine— toward which she had little knowledge or inclination, but she found his passion for them comforting. He was quite sure these things were worthwhile, and why not? As long as he didn't start voting Republican, she could tolerate some patrician pretensions in exchange for body warmth and decent chat. He was, despite his expensive coat, the rare man—person, really—who seemed to listen to her with something like full attention.

She wished her brother would come back from Mexico. When she'd visited him there the previous spring, she had insisted they visit a market she'd read about online, one that sold packets of ground-up bone wrapped in animal skin and statues of Jesus weeping blood and live birds and rabbits and snakes jammed into too-small cages. Philip hadn't wanted to go—he'd seen enough fucked-up things without having to seek them out, he said, and Cassie had, too, though not in Mexico—but once they were there, he gamely translated for her as she bargained. She was traditionally terrible at these kinds of negotiations, acquiescing to any market person willing to stand firm on a price for more than a few seconds. But her brother had developed some skill in his time here, it seemed, a toughness that came in handy now as she tried to secure a tiny metal sculpture of a flaming heart. She had no sense of its economic value, and it wasn't particularly beautiful. It had probably been produced in a factory. But she seized on the idea—and maybe it was subconscious and imposed retroactively—that it was important to concentrate her affection on one object in this overheated metropolis of things, even if it was arbitrary. Not caring overly much for the item she chose could be a statement that it was her attention itself that mattered, not what she chose to focus it on. Her brother got the heart down to what he deemed an appropriate price, with Cassie shaking her head along with his cues, even as her broad smiling throughout the interaction surely undercut him. Once they'd agreed, she sifted through the coins she'd pulled out of her pocket, attempting, with effort, to identify and add up the ones she needed. The woman in the stall seemed satisfied with the arrangement—she was offering to wrap her trinket in paper, place it in a dusty black plastic bag. "*No es necesito*," Cassie said, confident she was being understood. She would keep it somewhere on her person, loose. She'd chosen something small enough for that.

On the morning of a "personal day" that she'd decided she deserved, she woke up in Leonard's apartment after he'd left for work. She put the kettle on the stove to heat water for coffee and went to the bathroom to brush her teeth. On close examination, she was pretty sure that all of her teeth were rotting out of her gums. She emerged to the sharp smell of burning plastic. On the stove, the base of the kettle was on fire, its black, oh, shit, *plastic* melting like a hallucination into blue flames, smoke flowing enthusiastically toward the ceiling. She grabbed it by the handle and threw it into the sink, breaking the plate that had been waiting there patiently to be cleaned. The flames went out when she turned on the tap, but the entire apartment now smelled like a burned-down chemical plant. At least, she observed at a glance, the smoke detectors had been unscrewed; she saw one dangling by a wire above her head. She recognized now that she had, by lighting it on fire, destroyed what had until recently been a serviceable electric instant kettle. Cool, great. This was a very cool, great thing to do in one's newish boyfriend's apartment.

She went to the website of a monopolistic corporation that sold and quickly shipped objects for very low prices and found the same kettle in a slightly different color from the one she had ruined. It could be at the house *later the very same day* if she paid just a little bit more for it. So she did! She felt good about her decisiveness in tackling this problem. She couldn't remember the last time she had been so decisive. Even if the kettle arrived before Leonard came home and it looked exactly like the previous one, she told herself, she was *not* going to be sneaky and pretend it was the same kettle. She would admit blushingly to her mistake, but she would be funny about it, normal. "And it turned out they were selling the same one online for, like, zero dollars, basically!" she'd say. "Good thing you don't have expensive taste in kitchenware, ha ha!" She waited in the apartment all day for its arrival, watching from the window like a cat. When it arrived, in the late afternoon, she was disappointed. It was some kind of updated model that did not remotely match the picture on the website. She placed it exactly where the previous one had been but still planned— really, she wouldn't have a choice when he saw it—to tell Leonard what had happened. But a riddle for the ages unspooled over the subsequent weeks:

If an electric kettle is destroyed in a fire, and replaced by a kettle that looks nothing like it, and the longtime owner of said kettle does not notice the difference, is it possible, perhaps, that the original kettle was never really destroyed? Or: that it had never existed at all?

When her father came to visit her in Boston, he watched her eyes too carefully: for drink, for drugs, for signs that she had become angry with him again. When he'd divorced her mother, when she was eighteen, she'd been more for-giving than her brother, more willing to hear his side of the story, even if, ultimately, it had not proved particularly sympathy-inducing. She had known then, perhaps, that she was going to need to build up some credits for the psychic damage she was going to cause him with all the drugs. But now that she'd made it—for now—through what he referred to as her "difficulties," she found herself angry with him at random moments, furious about things he'd said and done more than a decade earlier, but that she hadn't been stable enough to do anything about at the time. She felt on some level that this wasn't fair of her. But she was also pretty sure that her father caught a lucky break in her having been too fucked-up to confront him when he most deserved it. Usu-ally now she felt a combination of tenderness and frustra-tion toward him, which seemed like the appropriate things for a daughter to feel toward her sixty-year-old father.

She'd taken him to dinner at a restaurant down the road from her apartment, a brilliant, dark little cavern operated by overgrown children who loved to put marrow and smoke into everything they made. Her father, with a sprightly multitude of tiny ingenious dishes to choose from, thought the burger sounded good. She ordered five things, to dem-onstrate how one should behave in this restaurant, and the burger as well, to appease him. He was wary of being tricked, she thought, by her and by the young people run-ning in and out of the open kitchen. She trusted the food here. Whatever they did—soaked everything in fat? spiked the water with MDMA?—the dishes came out tasting soft and wonderful, like the baby food of the future.

"I just want you to be happy," her father said.

He would love that she was dating Leonard, she knew that. Len was so completely her father's type that she was embarrassed to even mention him. Most of the men and women she'd dated were sweet-natured ruffians, artists and drug dealers and waiters, and her parents had treated them with varying levels of forbearance. But *this* fucking guy—more than gainfully employed, nice-enough-looking, drug-free except for Adderall all the time and weed on the weekends—fit their idea of the person she should be dating. She was almost mature enough, she thought, to not torpedo the relationship for that reason alone. But she also wasn't going to reveal her relative contentment and give her father the satisfaction of feeling right. He wasn't right; she'd gotten lucky. Another of his favorite phrases to repeat during her childhood: "I'd rather be lucky than good."

"I'm actually pretty happy right now," she said.

"You look tired," her father said.

Leonard, on one elbow in bed: "Do you think there's going to be a revolution?"

Cassie, on her back: "No."

She felt it a little more every day, the ebbing away of her rage at the president and his cabal of monsters. She hated them now with a colder certainty; she could vividly picture strangling various cabinet members without her pulse quickening. The desperation of the previous year had, she

realized, been tinged with something like joy, the catharsis of one's worst fears being realized. This current feeling, though easier to live with daily, was more like despair.
Of course they'd all gotten used to it, even if they claimed
they hadn't. Things for her were mostly the same as they
had been before. Better, in many cases, no thanks to the
shitheads running the country. One of her plays had been
named a finalist in a prestigious competition. Another was
going to have a staged reading in an experimental space in
a couple of months. Her substance intake was limited to
the occasional hits from Leonard's vape pen during long,
liquid nights of streaming video. Sure, she was worried all
the time that the world would soon be at war and that she'd
be dragged screaming and vomiting through the streets by
the police at the next protest she attended. But the anxiety
was tolerable. She could, to her relief and regret, live with
it. There was danger in projecting her own emotional vacil-
lations on the country at large, but, unfortunately for her
sense of herself as a unique and independent human, her
varying acceptance of the unending political crisis seemed
to map quite neatly onto that of her compatriots, or at
least—and crucially—those of her age and social position.
Re: Leonard's question, if there was going to be a revolution, it would likely come from roughly their quarter. And
the signs at the protests were still mostly jokes.

One night she took Leonard to the free night at the art mu-
seum. The lobby of the contemporary wing was a mess,

DJs playing terrible music, people waiting in long lines for . . . chips? Beer? Deeper inside there was a whole mini-exhibition dedicated to "stillness," to the notion of quiet contemplation as an important element in the life of the mind. She and Leonard were the only people there. There was tinkling piano music that turned out to be by John Cage, and, for some reason, a little room with blood-red walls hidden inside the gallery sheltering a mannerist painting of Christ coming down from the cross. Jesus filled most of the picture, his head poking out into the upper frame, his torso dominating the center of the painting. It certainly wasn't about stillness, and one of her least favorite things about paintings made before around 1800 was their insistence on depicting this particular execution with such grim relentlessness. But there was also a curly-headed angel in what looked to be a tie-dyed leotard, and he held a magnificently carved staff that was not un-phallic in nature.

"Well, I can get down with that angel," Cassie said.

"He's like, 'Oh hey, I was just wandering by,'" Leonard said.

"'Just saw somebody with an easel painting a dead guy and thought, well, shoot, I'm wearing my good outfit. Always *wanted* my picture done.'"

"Is it sacrilegious to make fun of angels?" Leonard said. "I feel that they're not, like, essential personnel."

"Yeah, no, it's fine," Cassie said. "They can't hear or talk."

"I didn't realize you were such a theologian."

"Oh yeah, it's harder to tell when I'm not wearing my . . . what, vestments? I'm trying to say 'robes,' but funnier."

These okay times they had, the banter and the looking and the judging, were enough to hold off the worst of it for a half hour or so. After that, more stimulation would be needed. It was exhausting, seeking the next thing. But she still knew all too well what was at the bottom of the pool. Maybe Leonard could teach her about watches? (How *did* one pronounce TAG Heuer?) She couldn't imagine caring about them as status symbols or even aesthetic objects, though she had become, she realized, pretty interested in time. She doubted that this was the point of engagement for him, but she liked the idea that they might share an enjoyment in the same thing for different reasons. He could pick the model and see to its maintenance. She—she would count the minutes.

At work, on a Friday, Eleanor finally called Cassie into her office.

"I know people have been talking, so you might have already heard something," she said.

"Oh," Cassie said. "I don't think so?"

Her hope for herself shifted to that of a more general, impersonal laying off—*cutbacks*, *quarterly reports*, other words she vaguely understood that might sever her from her job without it having been her fault.

"I'm retiring at the end of the year," Eleanor said. "It's a little complicated. I . . . well, I have my reasons, and they aren't all happy. You can probably guess pretty easily based on what's been happening here lately. But I wanted you to hear it from me."

Cassie did not know what had been happening there lately. Her attention had been squarely—justifiably, she thought, but still—on her own tentative hold on employment and sanity. There was a lesson here, maybe.

"Oh!" Cassie said. "I . . . congratulations?"

"It's complicated."

"Right," Cassie said. "Well, I know everyone will miss you. *I'll* miss you."

Eleanor turned over a book on her desk, studied the back, flipped it back onto its front.

"I guess, while we're here," Cassie said after another moment of silence. "Am I doing all right? At my job?"

Eleanor sized her up. The usual weighted disappointment was back in her eyes.

"I don't know, are you?" Eleanor said.

"I've been really trying," Cassie said. "I worry about it a lot."

"Well . . . if you weren't doing what you were supposed to do, start now. I'll give you a two-week head start. I think if you stop fucking around so much, you'll probably be fine."

Cassie was so relieved that she felt like a different person. It was like putting on a pair of glasses after years of blurred vision.

On her way out of the office, she accidentally caught up to Greta on the long walk to the T. Usually she tried to respect her coworkers' presumed desire not to speak to anyone from work after they'd clocked out, but she couldn't cross the street now to avoid her without it being awkward. Also, there was a cloud of sour smoke issuing from Greta's person, and this was something Cassie wanted to be a part of, even if only by proximity, even if it wasn't, strictly speaking, a great choice for her continued sobriety.

"Whatchoo doing?" Cassie said when she was a few feet behind her.

"*Mom*, it's *organic*!" Greta said. "You need a hit to start the weekend?"

"Sounds about right," Cassie said. She took a very dainty pull from the spliff, which was, she thought, surprisingly heavy on tobacco for a marijuana-delivery vehicle created by a child. It brought her instantly back to her college self, light-headed from cigarettes and lack of sleep, hunched in front of a box fan sending smoke out into the New York night.

"You don't really drink, right?" Greta said.

"Yep, kicked that shit," Cassie said. A mother pushing a stroller eyed them like the criminals they should have been.

"I feel like drinking is kind of whatever at this point," Greta said. "Like, culturally, it seems kind of over, you know?"

She was proud of her young colleague's confidence, but worried for her, too. How long would it be before the first major rupture in her life, the event that pulled her out of her youth and into whatever her life would become? (And how long before the next one for Cassie herself?)

"Alcohol makes me insane," she said, "but it's fine for

regular people. I like watching people have one or two drinks. After that I start to feel embarrassed for them."

"College in Boston scared me straight," Greta said. "I mean, straight*er.* I think there's maybe a quota of vomit that one can witness and still have a happy life, and I might have just about reached it. More?"

She held the spliff out between her fingers.

"Nah, I'm a one-hitter these days," Cassie said. "Cheap date."

Greta's eyes widened, whether in mockery or admiration, Cassie could not be sure.

On the train, she looked up from her book, as she always did while they crossed the Charles. It was half frozen, the water undulating discreetly around the blocks of ice, like cars swerving slightly, one by one, around a pothole. Was it doing that? Her language sometimes outpaced the available stimuli. Let it. The water was moving, and the ice was staying still. The train was moving, and she was perched solidly inside of it. It felt right. As the train descended back into the ground, she closed her eyes and waited for her stop.

Cool for America

I SNAPPED MY LEG IN TWO and lost the summer—six months on crutches and I'd be lucky if I didn't limp for the rest of my life. I went to the ground for a slide tackle in a pickup soccer game and felt what turned out to be my tibia shoot through my skin. I couldn't believe how fucking badly it hurt, and I must have conveyed that, since I spent the next three days on morphine. They sent me home all messed up and helpless but it's amazing how much trouble I got myself into anyway.

This was in Montana, where I taught a photography course in a summer program for gifted rural high schoolers in Missoula. (Show the kids the big city!) Even before the leg thing, the summer wasn't going well. I broke up with the woman I'd been seeing back East over some petty nonsense right before we were supposed to drive west together. She kept the puppy. I got through the drive with a twenty-five-disc audiobook of *Lonesome Dove*, by the end of which I was convinced Larry McMurtry was the American

Tolstoy. Then my rented house, in the part of town ominously designated the Upper Rattlesnake, was full of mice and mold, and there was an unadvertised pickup with no tires in the backyard. I drank myself to sleep and showed up to a classroom of seven dead-eyed teenagers. I distributed battered digital cameras, showed them the button to press, and sent them away with a self-portrait assignment. Then I went outside and joined the instructor-student soccer game.

Missoula has mostly treated me well in the four summers I've spent here and I don't want to come across like an asshole. But when I got hurt it was a real project to get anybody to come around and help me, even though the Rattlesnake is ten minutes from downtown. I couldn't drive, I couldn't teach, my leg hurt so much that at first I couldn't even use the crutches unless I desperately had to piss. On my second day home, Jim, a climbing instructor from Boston who'd gone native, left a Tupperware container of homemade granola at my front door with a note reading, "Get good, pal." For the next couple of weeks I got to know an older church lady one of my colleagues had tipped off to my existence. She brought pasta salad and told me that Ryan Zinke, with whom her cousin had gone to high school in Whitefish, had gotten a bum rap. On days when no one came around I tried to read through the haze of pain medication but it depressed the hell out of me. I ran out of cigarettes and didn't want to ask anyone to bring me more. I got lazy and pissed in bottles. I took pictures of the bottles.

One day during this rough patch there was an unscheduled knock at the door.

"It's open," I said. "If you're here to kill me I won't stop you."

"It's Chloe," the voice at the door said. "Jim's wife? I brought you a pizza and beer and some cigarettes."

I loved her, whoever she was. "You are an angel sent from God," I said.

She backed through the door with the stuff stacked on the pizza box. She was pretty in a messy way—dark hair piled up on her head, a sharp bent nose. I guessed she was a few years older than me, maybe mid-thirties. She was wearing ratty pink denim shorts that looked like they were about to fall apart. She put the pizza box down on the coffee table and opened the pack of cigarettes. She took one out and tossed the pack to me. "Do you smoke in here?" she said.

"Do I have a choice?"

She glanced around the musty room and into the kitchen. "You rented this place."

"Sight unseen," I said. "Should've kept it that way."

"Jim said you were funny."

"I'm really grateful to you for coming out here," I said. "You guys live nearby?"

"No, we're over on the north side, but I'm part-time at Rattlesnake Gardens," she said. "Almost no-time, lately."

"So I'm not tearing you away from your duties."

"Well, I'm missing *The Price Is Right*."

"You're welcome."

I wanted her to recognize my vulnerable position and, unbidden, lean over the couch and give me a delicate kiss. But we had a wonderful hour anyway. She was sympathetic but not full of shit, like a good teacher or police officer. In previous summers I'd had drinks with her husband and he'd helped me on the field when I got hurt. Now I knew he had excellent taste in women.

"I'm going to go home and take a run," Chloe said. "I'd invite you along, but . . ."

"I'm gonna be hearing shit like that the whole goddamn summer, huh?" I said.

"If you're nice to me."

My eyes followed her to the door like a well-trained dog's.

"Call when you need things," she said. "Don't be a pussy about it."

It was as if her coming by opened a lock of empathy in the hearts of my acquaintances. Chris brought me a card signed by everybody in the program and a bottle of whiskey. Mary Jo, the hip painting instructor, showed up with pot. Karen, a former student of mine who now lived in town, played Big Star songs on the ukulele and filled me in on Jim and Chloe.

"He totally doesn't appreciate her," she said. "He thinks he's such a stud because he's a climber and a biker and whatever but he doesn't realize he's just, like, cool for Missoula. She's cool for America."

"What's so bad about him?" I said.

"He doesn't give her enough attention," Karen said. "I always see him with his buds at the Union, drunk as shit on, like, a Tuesday. And it's, *Oh, Chloe's at home reading*, or *Chloe's at the movies*. It's depressing."

"You can't really understand anybody's relationship from the outside," I said.

"*I'd* totally get with her if she was into that," Karen said. "I wouldn't even feel bad about it."

The next week Jim and Chloe got me into the back of their Subaru and took me to the hospital for a checkup on my progress. I felt every bump in the road but I tried not to make too much noise.

"I remember when I broke my ankle on a climb," Jim said. "Getting back to camp was a bitch and a half. But I had to do it, you know? I put a stick in my mouth to bite down on when the pain got bad."

"Maybe you were a dog in another life," Chloe said.

The news at the hospital wasn't good. The bone hadn't been healing properly and they were going to have to do surgery. I'd have to rest the leg for another three months and do serious PT.

"Look on the bright side," Chloe said. "If you were a horse they'd have put you down a long time ago."

We went back to my house and Chloe and Jim decided the only thing to do in the face of my bad news was to throw a party. I would hold court on the couch and everyone would celebrate around me. Calls were made; beer was brought. My summer colleagues straggled by, along with grad students I'd never seen before. Some of them even talked to me.

"Do you like it better here or in Tennessee?" said a chubby guy in black-frame glasses. I had a tolerable assistant professor gig at a small college there, where I taught "intro to craft" courses and the occasional Harry Callahan elective.

"Usually here," I said. "But stuck on a couch in the mountains is worse than stuck on a couch in the South. Out here I'd usually be outside taking pictures of roadkill and shit. Back home I'd be on the couch anyway trying to stay cool. I don't even have neighbors to stare at."

"You could have been *Rear Window*," the guy said.

"I'm more into front-door action myself," I said.

"Are you on drugs or something?"

I drank a little more on top of my pain meds and things got funky. There were these *people* all over my house for no reason. They were out back sitting on the rusty pickup and crowded in the living room dancing a little. It felt like hours since I'd seen Chloe, whose fault all this was. Then she was at the foot of the couch, up at the edge of the cushion to avoid my swollen leg. She didn't seem drunk but I got the sense that she was lit up somehow, different. Something was activated in her.

"Have you always lived in Montana?" I said.

"I grew up in Helena," she said. "And made it all the way to Missoula."

"You could conquer the eastern states," I said. "With your legs and everything."

"Probably," Chloe said. Then, a couple moments later: "Jim's not a bad guy. He knows what he's about. He's not trying to be something else."

"What would you say he's 'about'?" I said.

"Climbing. Working hard," she said. "You might think

he's kind of full of shit but he's not. He came all the way out here to follow his passions, you know?"

"I liked him better before I knew you existed," I said.

Chloe leaned across the couch and rubbed my head. "Aw, it wishes I was single," she said.

I watched somebody's black Lab fending off the nipping of a mutt puppy on the floor.

"Maybe when you're all fixed up we can talk," she said. "As it is you'd be a sitting duck."

I went in for the surgery at St. Patrick a week later and it seemed to go all right, though it set me back on the movement front. It was now July and I wouldn't be able to travel for a few months, so I took a leave of absence from the fall semester back East. After a week at home, I got bored enough to ask the head of the program if I could teach my class from my house and she said yes. Apparently Chris had been "teaching" Vietnam movies while filling in for me and she was already getting emails from parents. So that Tuesday the high schoolers sat cross-legged around my couch and we talked about the photos they'd been taking. There was a lot of the usual—pictures of their feet, some blurry sub–Francesca Woodman mood shots—but there were a couple keepers. One girl had taken a series of pictures with her friends in tourist poses in which she'd deliberately put her finger in front of the lens. Another had taken photos of small children wearing her clothes.

"What do we think this is all about?" I said.

"They're her inner child?" a guy said.

"Good," I said.

I sent them home with a handout from Susan Sontag and instructions to take a photo of "some social significance." That'd keep 'em busy. I felt so good to be teaching again that I invited Chloe and Jim over to smoke and drink beer and watch Buster Keaton movies. Halfway through *The Navigator*, Jim said he wasn't interested in silent movies and went off to the bar.

"Be good," he said. Was this an Arthurian morality test?

"You don't have to stay," I said to Chloe. "Buster'll keep me company."

"Naw, this is tight," she said. "Chaplin without the bullshit."

We smoked a joint and had some more drinks and watched *Sherlock Jr.* It had gotten late and Jim hadn't called about picking her up.

"He's probably just drunk," Chloe said. "Like me."

"Well, you can take my car if you're all right to drive," I said.

"I shouldn't. But hey, there's a bed upstairs you can't get to, right?"

"Not even if I crawled," I said. "There's sheets and stuff in the closet."

"Sleep well," she said, getting up. "Don't dream about me."

When I woke to sunlight there was a note on the floor in front of the couch: "Never came so hard in my life. Let's do it again sometime. Yrs in Christ, the Navigator."

I spent the day emailing Tennesseans and trying not to think about Chloe. My mother called and pledged to visit soon; I advised against. My friends and colleagues had worked out some kind of rotation to attend to me (the details of which I could not follow), so I was not surprised to hear someone coming in the door that afternoon. But I was surprised that it was Jim.

"Howdy," I said. This was not something I said.

"Hey, buddy," he said. "Figured I'd take Chloe's shift today. Since she was here so late. Or early, I guess."

"Yeah, she crashed upstairs," I said. "I thought it was better than crashing my car."

"I appreciate that," Jim said. "I was in no condition myself."

I became aware then that Chloe's note was still there on the floor. I decided that God would not let it be seen.

"You get up to anything in particular last night?" I said.

"Some asshole got his ass kicked by a bouncer at the Rose for fucking with some girl's drink. It seemed real excessive."

"Whatever happened to the code of the mountains?" I said.

"Like the code of the sea and the code of the jungle, it may never have existed at all," Jim said.

He was now standing nearly on top of the note, which I prayed was facedown. He tossed me a pack of cigarettes and took the groceries into the kitchen.

"Look, man, there *is* something I wanted to talk to you about," he said. He was standing directly behind the couch, so I had to crane my neck back to see him. "I know how Chloe can be with guys sometimes and I don't consider you a threat or whatever. But this is a friendly reminder to keep things cool, all right?"

"I live on a couch," I said.

"Gotcha," he said. "You know, we're taking the students floating tomorrow."

"Flip a punk for me, yeah?" I said.

Jim's visit got me thinking, a real rarity. I'd spent years of my life getting educated—college, graduate school, those audio guides at the art museums—and now I was a teacher myself, but I still didn't really believe in it, at least not in the visceral way that some people believe in Jesus or supply-side economics. The pursuit of unavailable women was the closest I could get to a life's passion.

In the afternoon I attempted to assemble an Adirondack chair I'd ordered from Amazon. There weren't too many pieces—it looked like you could just jam the joints into the shape of a chair and be set. You couldn't. After half an hour I was covered in sweat and my good leg had cramped from the ridiculous position I'd contorted myself into. I left the shit in a pile and forgot about it until Chloe sauntered in the next morning wearing a sundress.

"Bad week," she said. "I wish someone would just pay me to be myself."

"I would if I wasn't so damn broke," I said.

"Jim talk to you?"

"He was concerned that I not get the wrong idea," I said. "Which I respect."

"I thought I could count on you to think independently." She knelt down in front of the couch so that we were eye to eye. "I'm pretty bored with things."

"Flattering as that is . . ." I said.

"Don't tell me you're not that kind of guy," Chloe said.

"I'm not a *kind* of guy," I said. "I'm a unique fucking snowflake."

"I just mean I don't think you're the type of guy who gets someone's interest up and just leaves them hanging."

She leaned over and kissed me.

"See?" she said.

"Yep," I said.

She kissed me again and then stood and straightened her back. She stared at the mess of would-be chair next to the couch.

"My pop was an accountant," I said. "It's not my fault I'm useless."

"This came out of a box," she said. "It has, like, five pieces. I'll just do it now."

"I thought we were doing something else," I said.

"We are," she said. "You'll appreciate this more later."

She knelt down over the wooden planks and started fitting them together without looking at the directions. Her hair was loose and hung down straight over her face when she bent over. When I caught a glimpse of her green eyes they were narrowed with focus, and she licked her lips as she worked. She was done in fifteen minutes and the chair looked goddamn perfect.

"Now take it apart for me and do it again blindfolded," I said.

"Greedy," she said, and left.

That evening I got Karen to drive me into town and brought along some Percocet. We had big plans—dinner, and, God willing, drinks. I felt all right while we ate, and the bar we went to afterward was sparsely populated. We set up camp with local IPAs in a corner booth.

"What's going on with you and Chloe?" Karen said.

"Nothing," I said.

"Fuck you, nothing," Karen said. "Jim's been going around saying he should kick your ass."

"If there *was* something going on, I wouldn't tell you," I said. "The first rule of having an affair is not to tell anyone you're having an affair."

"So you are."

"That's exactly what I didn't say."

My leg was starting to ache, but we'd just gotten there, and I needed to learn to deal with the pain. I looked up to see Chloe and Jim walking in.

"Small town," Karen said.

"Be cool," I said.

They spotted us and walked over. Jim extended his hand. "Look at you, out and about."

"I am risen," I said.

Chloe widened her eyes at me.

"We were gonna meet some folks but it doesn't look like they're here yet," Jim said.

"So have a beer with us?" Karen said, and kicked my good leg under the table.

"That'd be great," Jim said. "If you don't mind."

"Of course," I said.

Jim went to the bar and Chloe sat down with us. She played with a strand of hair that had fallen into her face.

"Been reading anything good?" I said.

"I just read *The Razor's Edge*," she said. "I liked it except for the end."

"Sort of dated maybe," I said.

"I'm at the point where I only want to reread stuff I've already read," Karen said. "Why read something new when you know there's something you already like?"

"Because it gets tedious?" Chloe said. "Even if it's bad, at least it's something different."

Jim came back with three beers.

"This one's for whoever," he said. "Whichever one of you wants it first."

"What's going on with you, dude?" I said.

"I went climbing out at Kootenai yesterday," he said. "The big wall was open and it was perfect conditions. I brought a newbie and she did a great job belaying."

"I would never trust someone like that," Karen said.

"Oh, come on, it's the best feeling in the world," Jim said. "Your life in somebody else's hands."

"It's only in somebody else's hands if you mess up," Chloe said. "The first line of defense is not falling."

"Right, but I wouldn't trust myself not to fall," Karen said.

"That makes sense," I said. "I wouldn't, either. But I guess I understand why somebody might find that fun."

"Fitzgerald says that's the sign of a smart person," Jim said.

"Oh, you *did* go to college," Chloe said. Jim put his hand over hers. He probably got that from a Starbucks cup.

"I think the best option is just to be right," Karen said. "Even if you can't see the merit of the other argument or whatever. What matters most is being right."

"Ah, youth," Chloe said. "I remember when *I* thought you could be right about things."

"You're right about *some* things," I said. "Somerset Maugham, Buster Keaton. The Replacements. The things that matter."

"Those are the things that matter?" Jim said.

"To some people," I said. "Interesting people."

It wasn't in my best interest to fuck with Jim, but I couldn't help it. Back in college—my peak period of un-disguised contempt for others—I'd always had my bigger, stronger buddies around if I took things too far. Now I was on my own.

"I guess I usually have other stuff on my mind," Jim said.

"I'm sure," I said. "World hunger and such."

"You ever thought about not being such a fucking smart-ass?" Jim said.

"Thought about it, yeah," I said.

"Hey, guys," Chloe said. "Let's not get into dick measuring here."

"That's really more your thing, isn't it?" Jim said.

Chloe got up from the table and walked out the door.

"Hey, nice work, bro," I said, and took a sip of my beer. Jim reached out and punched my glass into my front teeth. I heard a hollow *thunk*. The glass dropped heavily onto the table, intact. I tasted blood in my mouth.

"What the fuck, Jim?" Karen yelled.

I tongued my front teeth. One of them felt broken.

"You need to stay away from us," Jim said.

"You know where I'll be," I said through the blood.

The old-timers at the bar stared at me like cattle as Jim brushed past them. Just another night in the old saloon, I guess. I held a cocktail napkin to my mouth and called a dentist Karen found in her smartphone. He said to come in the morning. As I gimped my way out the door I looked up and down the block for Jim. No sign of him.

Back at my house Karen asked if I needed anything; I told her I needed to be alone. I took three Percocets, poured myself some whiskey, and lay down on the couch.

Some time later I heard somebody knocking. I'd actually locked the door, for the first time that summer. "It's Chloe."

I thrust myself up onto my working leg and opened the door a crack. "Where's Jim?" I said.

"Jim's dead," she said.

"*What?*"

"Not really. I don't know where Jim is. Can I come in?"

"You really shouldn't be here," I said. "You heard what he did?"

"He called to tell me," she said. "I hung up on his ass."

"Well, this is the first place he's gonna look," I said.

"If he comes here I'll call the cops," she said. "And he's already got a DUI. Just let me in. Please."

I locked the door behind her.

"Let me see," she said. "Jesus. Do you have the rest of the tooth?"

"No," I said. "Should I?"

"Sometimes if you have the rest of the tooth they can put it back together."

"It's just a tooth," I said.

She kissed my forehead, my nose, my chin. She went for my lips and I pulled away. My mouth felt like a swamp of bone and blood. She pushed my shoulders down slowly and I maneuvered myself into a sitting position. She unzipped my fly and pulled down my shorts. When she lowered herself onto my lap a sharp pain went through my leg. I tried to ignore it and concentrate on the mechanics at hand, but it seemed, in any case, that I'd taken too many Percocets to get hard. She tugged on me until it became unpleasant and I put my hand on her wrist to stop her. She gave me a tight-lipped smile and settled beside me on the couch. She made herself come, or at least pretended to, and rested her head on my shoulder. "That was nice," she whispered in my ear. I gave her a Percocet and she curled up and slept until the sun came through the big picture window.

"Damn, I've got to go home," she said.

"I don't know if you should do that," I said. "You want some breakfast?"

"What, Triscuits and mustard?" she said. "I'll be okay. Jim was just upset because you were being a jerk. Now I fucked you and you don't need to be a jerk anymore and things will settle down."

It occurred to me that I did not know or understand this woman.

"I've got a dentist appointment in a couple hours," I said.

"You know, I went to high school with these two girls, twins," Chloe said. "They both became dental assistants or hygienists or whatever, and they worked in the same office. So you'd go in and get your teeth X-rayed and it would be Amanda, and then you'd go sit in the chair to get your teeth cleaned and it would be Katherine They looked exactly the same, they both bleached their hair, they both wore those little white dentist coats. I always figure dentists are having sex with their assistants, you know, and you have to wonder what was going on with those two. I mean, they were doing stuff in the *chair*, probably, knowing them. This was back in Helena."

She gave me a hard kiss on the mouth—it hurt like a motherfucker—and went out the front door. I ran my finger over the jagged edge of my tooth. At least it had taken my mind off the leg.

I slept through my dentist appointment. Maybe if I left it broken it would make me look tough. The students came at two and circled around me in my new chair like I was Socrates, with a glass of whiskey instead of hemlock. We'd just started going over their socially significant photographs—a smiling homeless man by the river, a row of safety helmets on a fence in front of a closed-down mill—when Chloe came in the door and slammed it behind her. She went straight upstairs. I'd been looking forward to talking about the assignment but I couldn't concentrate on what the kids were saying. I let them go early without giving them anything for next week. When they were gone Chloe came down.

"Jim's freaking out," she said. "He wants to leave me."

"Do you think he will?" I said.

"Well, we were having problems *before* you came along,"

she said. "I don't know. Meeting you might have clarified some things for me. Like maybe I need to be with somebody more interesting, you know? Like you were saying."

I didn't like where this was going.

"All relationships have their rough patches," I said. "You might feel differently in a little while."

"Can I stay with you for a couple of days?" she said.

"I mean . . ." She was standing over me. The skin around her eyes crinkled like she was going to cry. I stared at the ceiling, my leg throbbing. "Of course you should stay. Obviously. For as long as you need to."

"Jesus, for a second I thought you were going to say *no*," she said. "I'm gonnna bring some stuff in from the car."

She went out, leaving the front door open. I watched her pull a suitcase and a duffel bag out of the backseat and set them down in the driveway. She leaned back into the car and emerged with a waffle iron piled high with paperbacks. She carried it into the kitchen without looking at me.

"I wish I could help," I said.

Short Swoop, Long Line

KATE'S TWO SONS, ENGULFED
in their hoodies, were waiting in line at the pizza counter behind Alex. It was startling to see them in person. Alex had never met them, only glanced at pictures of them around Kate's house when he slept over on nights when the kids were with their dad. In the pictures, they were smiling, their arms around their mother, sporting polo shirts and respectable haircuts. Dad was not in the pictures.

Now the sixteen-year-old wore all black. The younger one, thirteen maybe, was in camouflage. They weren't smiling anymore. They wore flat-brimmed baseball caps over shaggy skater curls and grim masks of teenage boredom. Alex ordered his slices and a local pale ale and sat down in a booth near the window. He opened *Tender Is the Night*, which was going quite slowly, and tried not to look over at the kids, who, of course, sat down at the table next to his.

"Yo, can I get that Parmesan?" the older one said, suddenly looming over him. Jason, that was his name. Alex passed it to him.

"Thanks," Jason said. Then, under his breath, he added: "Faggot."

Alex tried to make his face look stern, like a disappointed adult. Jason and the little one—Matthew?—covered their mouths and mimed silent laughter. Alex was a twenty-four-year-old bookstore manager, which made him twenty-two years younger than Kate, the kids' mother, who, she'd made clear, was not his girlfriend. He was too old to pick a fight with her children, but still young enough to feel the sting to his pride. The fact that he could say "I'm having sex with your mom," the ultimate adolescent trump card, gave him some peace. The fact that he could also say "I've been wearing your mom's panties all week," and "I recently spent the night under your mom's bed at her request," was maybe more ambiguously triumphant for their age group.

He read and listened to the boys discuss an episode of *South Park* in which the citizens of South Park are plagued by a sound that makes them uncontrollably flatulent. When the kids got up to leave, Alex looked up from his book.

"You know, guys," he said. "It's not cool to commit hate crimes against random strangers."

"Stop checking out my dick, dude," Jason said. Matthew giggled and looked at Alex expectantly.

"I know your mother," Alex said.

"Cool, bro," Jason said. He inexplicably switched to a terrible British accent. "You probably shouldn't tell her you were examining our willies, mate."

"Oy, mate!" Matthew added, in an even less accurate accent. "Oy! You're fatter than Batman!"

They threw their plates in the trash and walked out of the restaurant.

Alex and Kate had started sleeping together three months earlier, after meeting at a scantly attended honky-tonk concert at the VFW Hall on Main Street. Kate was the executive director of a women's health nonprofit in town, and Alex heard her "community connection" PSA on the local NPR station twice a day. He told her, numerous times, that she was "too hot for radio"; she had a freshly bleached, very short haircut and tall boots. She was in the process of divorcing her husband due to a "whole truckload of bullshit," and she'd talked to Alex at length about that, and about her recent obsession with Scandinavian crime fiction, and Gillian Welch, until the bar closed. Then she'd surprised him by inviting herself back to his messy apartment out by the Walmart. Once there, she ordered him to his knees. It was a strenuous, educational night, significantly more demanding than his previous casual encounters. He drove her back to her car in the morning.

"Is that how things usually go with you?" he said.

"Boy, you have no idea," she said.

Alex had assumed this was a one-shot deal, something to be brought up in a drunken bout of sexual trivia someday. But instead, they started spending a few nights a week together, at his place or at her empty new rental on the north side. Kate, straddling his chest, said he was "boy cute," and praised his pliant body, which was flattering since he had started on a serious beer gut and was careless about his grooming. She had very specific notions about the tenor of their relationship—she was *having new kinds of fun* in the wake of her marriage's collapse.

Once she was done working him over, Kate asked him questions about his friends and ex-girlfriends and family, even though he saw his life as a minor farce compared to hers, with the soon-to-be-ex-husband, the budget cuts at her organization, her mother in a long-term care facility, the kids crashing toward and through puberty. She chided him for thinking that way. "Your problems aren't less valid just because you're young," she said. Except, of course, that they were.

A couple of nights after the pizza shop incident, Alex was at Kate's place, reading Cynthia Ozick essays at the kitchen island while she made spaghetti sauce.

"You doing anything fun this weekend?" she said over her shoulder.

"My dad's visiting, actually," he said.

"Oh, *that's* fun," Kate said. "Am I gonna get to meet him?"

"Do you want to?" Alex said.

"I wouldn't mind," she said. "Unless it would make you a worried little puppy."

He thought about this. There were a couple of levels of difficulty. He didn't want to ask Kate to clarify their relationship, for fear of messing with a good thing. But he was also wary of her interacting with his father while they occupied this ambiguous sexual space. He didn't care for Kate to be a subject of contemplation for his father at all, really.

"It would be fun if it works out," he said, diplomatically, he hoped. She was silent. He stumbled forward, trying to move past the subject.

"I saw your kids at Good Pie the other day," he said. He regretted it before it was all the way out of his mouth.

"Oh?" she said.

"Yeah, they sat down right next to me," he said.

"And did you . . . interact with them?"

"Well . . ." The die was cast, if that was the right saying. "Jason called me a faggot," he said.

"*What?*"

"That was a joke," he said.

"No, seriously, Alex, what did he say?"

"He asked me for the red pepper, I passed it to him. He said, 'Thanks, homophobic slur.' "

Kate turned back to the pot of sauce.

"I mean, I could have misheard."

"Jason doesn't like red pepper," she said quietly.

"Look, it's not a big deal," Alex said. Why had he lied about the condiment?

"You're telling me my son is going around saying hateful things to strangers."

"I'd like to think he's just misinformed," he said.

She shook some oregano into the sauce and then went to the sink.

"You shouldn't be talking to them," she said.

"I'm sorry I brought it up," Alex said. "They're great-looking kids."

"Yeah, I know," Kate said.

She started chopping vegetables and Alex stared at her back over the top of his book. She was wearing a tight faux-leather skirt that Alex couldn't be sure was intended for his appreciation. Of course, he shouldn't have mentioned the boys. File under shit you don't learn by dating twenty-two-year-olds.

They ate dinner sitting side by side on the couch, their plates resting on the coffee table that Alex had cleared of her books for the occasion. Kate had lived here for three months but refused to decorate it or even unpack all the boxes, since it was only supposed to be until the divorce settlement was finalized, when she would "have a better idea of the ol' finances." The clutter helped bridge the age gap for Alex; he felt comfortable in squalor.

"I want to see that violent Ryan Gosling movie," Alex said after five minutes of silence.

"I can't remember the last time I even *went* to the movies," Kate said.

"We should do it," Alex said.

"Movies are expensive," she said. "And usually terrible."

He put his hand on her knee, and she looked down at it, then back up at him, before shifting away.

"I thought it would be weird not to mention your kids," he said.

"Right," she said. "Because you're a baby and have no manners. If I wanted a mature, concerned boyfriend, I'd get one."

She had never spoken to him this way outside of the bedroom, and he wondered disconsolately whether this was the way she actually saw him. His only plausible weapon now was silence, so he ate his pasta and stared at a pile of books on the floor. On top was a collection of stories about "the West" that a friend of his had told him was "the worst book ever written." As a result, Alex had never read it. There were a lot of books like that. He wished, sometimes, for a less mediated life.

When they finished eating (Kate had stared at a week-old copy of the *Times Magazine* for the second half of the meal), Alex collected their plates and took them to the sink.

"I've got some work I need to do tonight," Kate said from somewhere behind him.

"How am I supposed to interpret that?"

"That I'm not going to fuck you," Kate said. "And not in a fun making-you-wait way, either."

"I guess I'll leave, then," Alex said. "I didn't come here to wash dishes."

"Good, you're terrible at it."

This had escalated fast. He'd been pretty sure he'd be able to work things back around to getting laid. Now it looked like this friendship, relationship, whatever, might be ending.

"I'm going home," he said. "I'm sorry, I guess. Or not. I don't know what I thought this was."

She cocked her head, a mirrored pantomime of him thinking. He walked out of the kitchen and out the front door to his car. In the passenger seat was the clean shirt he'd brought to wear the next day. It was only just starting to get dark out.

Two nights later, he sat on his front porch after work, drinking a beer. It was his fourth fall here and he couldn't imagine getting sick of the evening light. He'd come to town as a transfer student at the university after two years of misery at Amherst, where both his parents and three of his cousins had gone. He hadn't been able to deal with all the New England horseshit—the Barbour coats, the sports, the interest in the goddamned *leaves*. Plus, he was on the verge of failing out. On a trip home, a pothead friend from high school rambled at him about how state schools in the West loved out-of-state underachievers because they were usually willing to pay the hiked-up full tuition. Alex applied to the universities of Montana, Colorado, and New Mexico without telling his parents. When he finally told his father that he'd gotten into UM, his father told him he was disappointed that he wouldn't graduate from Amherst, but not about paying twenty-five grand a year less for his education.

And, surprise, in a direct rebuke to American good sense, getting two thousand miles away from Massachusetts brought out a latent interest in literature and philosophy. The weed was better, the beer was cheaper, and he had teachers who were impressed by what he'd picked up in his previous years of overeducated sleepwalking. He managed to talk his way into some master's seminars in English and film—"Women's Pictures: Pym, Stanwyck, and the Uses of Melodrama"—and graduated with good grades and moderate camping skills. He stuck around town doing what there was to do, stocking shelves at the organic grocery store, hustling the occasional band profile for the alternative weekly. When the lone full-time employee of the small bookstore followed his girlfriend to Seattle, Alex was the first person the owner called, since he was the only customer under forty who bought hardcovers on a regular basis. He'd been writing staff picks and restocking the shelves now for a year, despite his father's biweekly pleas for him to come back East and get a real job, or at least go to law school.

And he did still feel the melancholy of being far from home, the huge, teeming country between him and everyone he'd grown up with. He spent his Sunday mornings watching football games alone at the cinder-block dive in the center of town, regretfully eating two to seven slices of the free pizza provided by the guys from the Philadelphia-themed sub shop across the street. He would order something easy on the stomach to start—a Miller Lite, maybe—and work his way up to the hearty local beer by halftime. He'd smoke cigarettes outside at commercial breaks with the scruffy guys in hunting gear, looking at the photographs of large, dead animals on their phones and resisting the urge to snicker at their outsized pride. Together, they watched the college girls following their own weekend rituals, some in sweaters on their way out to brunch with their parents, others disheveled in skirts and heels, still trying to put an end to the night before. Watching them, only two years out himself, he found himself grateful that he had made it through that part of his life alive and relatively unscathed.

Now his father was due for a visit, his first since Alex

had moved to Montana. He wasn't dreading his father's arrival, exactly, but he also wasn't quite sure what to do about it. His parents had gotten divorced soon after he left for Missoula, and Alex had maintained a cordial, if not overly warm, relationship with his father, visiting him for meals and holidays but usually sleeping at friends' houses. He'd consistently encouraged his father to visit, in vague terms, with the fairly doubtful promise that if his father *saw* it out here, he'd understand the appeal. His father was not the outdoor type, though he'd been a Boy Scout, and thus thought of himself as a person who appreciated nature. He was most appreciative of nature when it could be quickly followed, or, preceded, by a decent glass of Pinot Noir. (The same was admittedly true of Alex, though man of the people that he'd become, he preferred a shot and a beer.) Luckily enough, Missoula had recently been blessed—cursed?—with its first fancy wine bar. Alex was torn, in his imagining of the visit, between his desire to show off the town's timid flickerings of culture and wanting to drag his father to one nightmarish hovel he frequented after another. You call yourself a Republican? Welcome to the real America, *Dad*. It's full of cheap shit and alcoholics. He would probably strike some kind of balance, like a sucker. His phone buzzed and Kate's face flashed on the screen.

"I'm sorry I got nasty the other night," she said. "I'm stressed, you know?"

"It's fine if you don't want to hang out anymore," he said. "I'm going to be pretty busy for a while."

"Oh, I'm *sure*," she said. "I'm just glad I got my shot."

"I mean, I'm not *going* anywhere," he said.

"Okay."

"Do you want to hang out?"

"Well," she said. "I did think we were having fun until things got off track."

He didn't know whether this was genuine solicitude or an elaborate, backhanded way of dictating his actions. In any case, it had quickly worn down his resistance.

"I'm free tonight, actually," he said. "Should I come to you?"

"You could come now," she said. "Or, well, how about this: Come. Now."

The next evening, Alex put his car in short-term parking—it would cost him two dollars at most—and waited in the small airport for his father's plane to arrive. It was a half hour late, and he stood in the arrivals area reading D. H. Lawrence and glancing up at the television showing CNN. Breaking news: cable news was fucking terrible.

Finally, the arrivals board signaled an arrival, and a few minutes later a small stream of wary visitors emerged from a set of automatic doors. Alex's father was in his customary traveling uniform: wool sport coat, button-down shirt, and pressed khakis. He was trailing at a polite distance behind a large, slow-moving man in an oversized T-shirt and baseball cap. His father's shock of remaining hair was whiter than Alex remembered it and he was, very uncharacteristically, wearing a pair of rimless glasses instead of contact lenses. He gave Alex a tired, grateful smile upon recognition.

"Oh, hello there, son," he said, stepping into Alex's

one-armed hug. The brief scrape of his father's stubble against his cheek set off a burst of childish, slightly unwelcome affection.

"Good to see you," Alex said. "How was the trip?"

"To tell you the truth, I wouldn't have minded a bigger plane on that last leg," he said. "*Little* bit tight. But, overall, not *too* too bad. At least I can say I've seen the Salt Lake City airport."

"You look good," Alex said. He *did* look good, or fine, at least. He didn't *not* look old, but: he wasn't not old.

"You, too," his father said. "Except for this hair . . . situation."

"It's the West, man. Don't be such a square."

Now that his father was before him, the idea of taking him to one of the dives in town revealed itself as the impossibility that it had always been. He would take his father to the nice-for-Missoula restaurants that he rarely patronized on his own. It was easy to forget, when he didn't see him for a while, that he might actually enjoy making him happy.

They drove out of the airport, down the lonely stretch of highway toward town.

"The air out here's really incredible," his father said. "Are those the mountains?"

"That's them," Alex said.

"Huh. I thought they'd be a little bigger."

"We have to drive a little bit to see the big boys. Are you hungry?"

"*Oh* yeah. You have to practically *beg* for peanuts on the plane now."

He decided to take his father to the Robber Barons, a

spot favored by university faculty and grad students for its decent cocktails and bison burgers. It was also where he'd told Kate they would probably end up, if she felt like saying hi, as part of his extended apology for mentioning her children's terrible behavior.

They were seated and talked about baseball for a few minutes, until it became clear that Alex didn't actually follow baseball anymore.

"So are you seeing anyone?" his father said.

"Nothing that serious," Alex said. "I've had a few Internet dates."

"You know, Ellen was saying the other day—and she's sorry, again, that she couldn't make it—that all of her friends are on dating sites now. Even"—he leaned in—"some of the *married* ones. Wild times, A."

"You think Ellen would be all right with you on a dating site?"

His father ran his hand over the top of his head.

"Oh, not me," he said. "I didn't mean . . . No, Ellen would *not* be happy about that." He'd been married to Ellen for three years now and they both treated her, conversationally, as a totemic figure.

"They have giant gin and tonics here," Alex said. "And they're really cheap if you get local spirits."

"Gin isn't supposed to be local," his father said.

This struck Alex as one of the more profound things his father had ever said. Still, he ordered a double Montgomery gin and tonic for himself. His father had a vodka martini, seemingly scared off of the idea of gin entirely. They talked pleasantly about the family—who was living where, which cousin had produced yet another grand-child for her grateful grandmother. Moments after they were served their burgers, Kate approached the table from deeper inside the restaurant. Had she been watching them this whole time?

"Alex*an*der, you didn't tell me your *brother* was coming to visit, too," she said. She gave a toothy smile.

"Shameless," Alex said.

His father smiled emptily, waiting to be told what was going on.

"Sorry, I'm Kate," she said. "I heard you were in town. Alexander's been a very dear friend to me during a difficult time."

"Tom," said Alex's father. "Yes, he can be moderately helpful when he wants to be."

There was a momentary hesitation, each of them a hair too polite to make the respective invitations and excuses required of them.

"Join us for a drink?" Alex's father said finally. "If you don't mind watching us eat."

"Oh, I don't want to interrupt your reunion," Kate said. "It was nice to meet you, Tom."

"No, no, stay," Alex said. "I'm trying to show my dad the best of Missoula. But you'll do for now."

He was thrilled to get another big-time smile out of this silliness, the first of those he'd provoked since she'd chewed him out the other night. He was pretty sure he wasn't in love with her—that would be pretty stupid, no?—but still, it was great when she smiled at him.

"So you're just here for the weekend?" Kate said.

"Wish it could be longer," said Tom. "I love it here already."

"I've been here for . . . God, almost twenty years," Kate said. "If you'd told me when I was a surly Boston teenager that I'd live in *Montana* for the length of my adult life, I'd have, I don't know, put my cigarette out in your eye or something."

"I still can't believe I live here, either," Alex said. "It seems like a weird dream sometimes."

"Don't put it in his head that he's going to stay for twenty years," his father said.

"It's a good place to raise a family," Kate said. Alex watched her face harden as she contemplated that.

"We miss seeing him, that's all," his father said to him. "The only reason your mother calls is to ask if I know when you're coming to visit."

"Well, it's good you're talking," Alex said.

"How long have you been divorced?" Kate said.

"Oh . . ." Tom said. "What? Four years? Five?"

"I'm in the process now," Kate said. "I can't even see the end of it."

"Not fun," Tom said. "Not . . . fun."

Alex checked his old, semi-dormant outrage at his father's callousness. Even though he'd been twenty years old when his father left his mother, he'd felt a buzz of betrayal that lasted longer than he thought was socially acceptable for someone of his age and political affiliation. He told himself, and others, that he was mostly upset on behalf of his mother, whom he'd seen treated unkindly. He remembered, while waiting for a flight home from the last vacation they all took together, his father berating his mother for reserving coach seats, returning again and again to how much pain his knee was going to be in as his mother pleaded with the ticket agent to change their seats. Eventually she had managed to get his father to the front of the plane, while she and Alex and his sister, Elyse, sat together in coach behind the inevitable screaming baby.

"I just can't believe he *hates* me so much," his mother said to them. "I know he's not happy, but why is he so *angry*?"

"It's just a midlife crisis," Elyse, sixteen, said, as if she had any idea.

In Alex's first semester at UM, he'd endured marathon phone sessions with his mother in which she raged operatically while he watched football games on mute to keep from losing his mind. He'd mostly ignored his father's calls, watching his phone jump while the voice mails piled up, only summoning the courage to listen to and delete them when they filled his in-box and prevented "new messages from being received," as a patient, recorded voice informed him.

Even when relations were at their worst, though—when his mother would not countenance the word *Dad* spoken in her presence, and Elyse had been too overwhelmed by the situation to attempt diplomatic outreach—he had, on winter break, gone alone to visit his father in his furnished, ridiculously expensive apartment downtown. They'd traded updates on old family friends and their children, then sat on a suede Crate & Barrel couch in front of an enormous flat-screen television for an entire meaningless college football game, drinking light beer and expensive wine, respectively, silent save to acknowledge a particularly aggressive hit or egregious call. On the dark, wooded drive back to his mother's house, he castigated himself for not confronting his father. He was embarrassed to feel so much, too embarrassed to express it. Of course, as everyone counseled him it would, time had taken the edge off of his feelings. And now he could feel guilty about that, too.

"So you guys are going to, what, go hiking?" Kate said now. "Fishing? Do you *fish*, Alexander?"

"Never," he said. "I haven't even read *A River Runs Through It*."

"It's actually really good," Kate said. "I mean, I don't think it's just Stockholm syndrome. Missoula syndrome."

"How do you two know each other again?" Tom said. It seemed that something in their familiarity had suddenly tipped him off. Alex caught Kate's eye. He felt like he was blushing, though he wasn't sure his face actually did that.

"I'm a bookstore fiend," Kate said, which happened to be true. "I think fifty cents of every dollar I spend is at Marlowe's."

"Yeah, most of the money they pay me just goes right back in the register," Alex said.

"I have to say, Tom, for someone his age . . ." Kate said. "How old are you again, A?"

She knew exactly how old he was.

"Twenty-four," he said.

"Wow, twenty-four," she said. "Jesus. For someone his age—I mean, *any* age—he's incredibly well read. Are you a big reader, Tom?"

His father finished his martini and rolled the olive into his mouth, chewed for a moment, and swallowed.

"Nonfiction," he said. "I read some history when I have time. Biographies. I don't know where Alexander got his, ah, bent."

"My mother's an English teacher," he said.

"Right, I meant besides that," his father said. "Obviously."

"Neither of my boys likes to read," Kate said. "It kind of breaks my heart, but I'm holding out hope that they'll come around."

"Well, Allie took his time getting started," Tom said. "Little bit of a rough patch. But he got through it."

"Mostly I just fucking hated Amherst," Alex said to Kate. His father's face fell. He looked younger when he was pouting, for some reason.

"You never know what's going to be the thing that inspires you," Kate said. "I thought I was going to be a modern dancer in New York and I ended up running a nonprofit in Montana."

"Right," Tom said. He wasn't really listening. He was looking for the waitress. He'd been wounded by the one-two punch of talking about his ex-wife and the Amherst dig. Okay, Dad.

"Should we go to that new wine place tomorrow?" Alex said brightly, like one would offer a walk to a sulking dog. "There's this new wine place that's supposed to be really good."

"You haven't been?" Kate said, catching on to the need for a change of tone. "It *is* good. As long as you don't mind a little bit fancy."

"Well, I don't know if I packed for *fancy*," Alex's father said, glancing vaguely down at his torso.

"You're wearing a sport coat," Kate said. "You could be the *mayor* of this town by morning."

"All right, then," Tom said. "Twist my arm. Wine bar tomorrow. I'm going to hit the men's. If you find the waitress . . ." He snapped his credit card down on the table. "Make sure they include your friend's drink, too."

As he walked away, Kate put her hand over Alex's.

"Just imagine how bad it would be if you *weren't* here," he said.

"You're really lucky," Kate said. "Some people have really shitty parents."

"You don't know the whole story," he said.

"Yeah, yeah," she said. "I'm just telling you, objectively speaking. You got a good deal."

"Sure," Alex said. "I'm a solvent white American."

"You're not that white," she said. She removed her hand and sat back. "Dad at four o'clock. Or, well, something o'clock. Give me a text when you guys are done, okay?"

When Tom sat back down, he put on his reading glasses and held the check close to his face, then put it back down on the table. Alex watched him add a generous tip, then scrawl a signature identical to his own. Short swoop, long line.

"I hope we see you again," Tom said as they all exchanged hugs in front of the restaurant.

"Well, I'm around," she said. "You guys have fun tomorrow. Watch out for bears!"

"Really?" Tom said.

"Naw," Alex said.

There really were a lot of bears.

He drove his father toward his hotel out on Reserve. He'd offered to let him sleep on his pull-out couch, but Tom had turned him down, and Alex was glad he hadn't had to make his place clean enough to host a parent.

"That was a good pick," Tom said. "Good food. And, I have to say, your friend Kate is very cool."

"She's great," Alex said.

In the silence that followed, Alex was seized by the urge to tell his father about their relationship, or whatever it was. But he couldn't bring himself to breach that gulf. Let his father think he had a chance; or let him suspect, if only in the very back of his mind, what his son was up to.

"She's my favorite person in this town," Alex said.

He kept his eyes on the road but he felt his father's glare in his peripheral vision. Alex turned and caught his eye for a moment.

"I'm looking forward to the grand tour," his father said finally.

Alex pulled up in front of the hotel. He unbuckled his seat belt and leaned across the car's center console to hug his father, who hugged him back harder than he expected him to, harder than he had in a while.

"Be good," he said.

Kate carried two glasses of bourbon on ice into the living room. She'd changed into a sheer purple negligee thing, the kind of thing that Alex had only seen in the display window of Victoria's Secret. She was playing the new D'Angelo album through her laptop speakers, and Alex got caught up in it, even in that tinny state.

"Family stuff stressful?" she said.

"I didn't think so," he said. "Do I seem stressed?"

"Preoccupied," she said.

Alex took a sip of his drink. It was much better than that lousy gin and tonic he'd insisted on having at the restaurant.

"Do you *like* me, Kate?" he said. "I don't mean *love* or anything. But do you, like, *like* me?"

"Aw, little baby," she said. "What's the matter?"

"I don't mean for it to be a thing," he said.

"Do you think I like your dad?" she said.

"I definitely didn't say that," he said.

"He's sweet," she said. "I mean, he's got an ego, obviously. But so do I. I imagine we'd get along under other circumstances. You're lucky you've still got all your hair."

She ran her hand through it, kissed his neck. He was vaguely ashamed at being easily turned on. But maybe, if looked at from a certain angle, *he* was the one who had the power. Because *he* was the one being acted upon, which made him the necessary *medium* for power, something like that. He was overthinking it. He didn't have to make a decision about how he felt about any of this right now. That was something he'd only just figured out. It helped with sex, keeping an open mind. It was *better* to be led. Acted upon.

"Time for bed," Kate said after a few more minutes. She took his hand and he followed her up the stairs, past the framed family pictures he didn't particularly care to see. The kids belonged to her, he thought, like he belonged to his father, if he still did. At a certain age the roles reversed. But, lord willing, that wouldn't be for a while.

She kissed him again at the bedroom door.

"You good?" she said.

"Like you care," he said.

He tried to look serious as they sat down on the bed.

In the morning, Kate woke him from a dream of an apocalyptic road trip.

"Time to go, boychik," she said. "Kids are due and you've got to show your dada Big Sky Country."

"Noooooo," he said.

"Don't make me get the spray bottle," she said. "C'mon."

Alex collected his clothes from the floor and put them back on slowly. His father had told him that, despite the presence of five local coffee shops in town, he strongly preferred to begin his day at Starbucks. There was one out on the highway in the vicinity of his father's hotel—he would take him there on their way out to the valley where he liked to hike, a stretch that was picturesque but not too steep, undamaged but not too remote. Plus there was a brewery nearby.

He trundled downstairs feeling unwashed and sleepy.

"*Kate*, I need *coffee*," he said in a parody of a whiny child.

Her two boys were standing in the living room, a duffel bag and backpack over their shoulders, respectively, staring at him with their dead eyes.

"Uh, *Mom*?" the older one called toward the kitchen.

"No worries," Alex said. "I'm just on my way out."

The kids remained in place, impassive. At the front door, Alex turned back and saw Kate coming out of the kitchen, drying her hands on a towel, a rigid smile on her face.

"Guys, this is Alexander," she said. "He's just . . ."

"Your *boyfriend*?" the little one said.

Alex caught her eye, took his hand off the doorknob.

"Oh *no*, honey," she said, playacting, he hoped, disgust. "He's my friend's son."

The kids looked at Alex uncertainly, the little one with the parakeet head-tilt he'd clearly picked up from his mother. It was not at all clear to Alex how this served as a reasonable explanation for his presence in their house at 8:00 a.m., but it seemed to have at least diverted their attention.

"Have a good day," Kate said. "Tell your dad I said hi."

The older one fell into an armchair with a sigh and took out his phone. The little one wandered toward the kitchen without saying anything. Satisfied enough, or already bored. Both.

"You need breakfast, Matt?" she said. She gave Alex a small nod and followed her son out of the room. Alex opened the door and then paused at the threshold.

"'Bye, Jason," he said.

The kid was still staring at his phone.

"Yes, he's rather a *fat* Batman, I do say," Jason muttered in a British accent, not looking up.

"Listen," Alex said.

This, *this* would be the moment to tell the kid what was really going on with him and Kate, to lay some truth on him. It was an awful generational cliché, but really: the kid still hadn't looked up from his fucking phone! The roof could come down and Jason wouldn't notice. He wouldn't even know if Alex walked out the door without finishing his sentence. And, in fact, that was the only adult option available.

He'd been on this hiking trail at least a dozen times, but he knew his father would be impressed by it, and he was feeling a stronger-than-usual desire for his approval. He wondered if his father wanted to strangle his stepchildren the way that Alex wanted to strangle Kate's kids. Probably more, but in a different way, since he actually knew them, and the feeling was probably tempered by the fact that he was a sixty-year-old man who had raised two children of his own, and knew, maybe, not to let them wield power over him.

Walking alongside and a little behind his father, he remembered Tom's rare bursts of unbridled anger. Once, as a child, Alex had found a new Pirates hat, tag still attached, sitting on the kitchen table. Assuming it was a gift for him, he'd put it on and spent the afternoon running around the yard wearing it while kicking a soccer ball with his sister. When he came in for dinner, he thanked his father for the gift, and was unsettled by the stony expression on his face. The hat had been meant as a gift for his cousin's birthday. How many hats and shirts and everything else did he already have? Why would he take something without asking? And then *ruin* it? He'd handed the hat to his father and gone to his room crying, not coming down for dinner despite his mother's coaxing. It was too much—the humiliation of having believed he deserved something he didn't, the scowl in return for his good-kid gratitude. He didn't want to *live*. When he finally crept downstairs, to the rest of the family watching television without him, his father silently got up and microwaved him a Hot Pocket. A Hot Pocket! Why didn't he give him leftovers? Was it an apology? Further punishment? He loved Hot Pockets, but even he knew that they weren't really dinner. Then they all watched *Frasier* like nothing had happened.

He wondered what he imagined all kids wondered about their parents—did they *forget* their cruelties, their accidental bursts of raw emotion? Or did they just try to cover them up in the hope that the kid, the sieve-headed nonentity, might be the one to forget? Probably, Alex knew now, nobody forgot, and life accumulated these misunderstandings until somebody died. Kate had said that his father wasn't so bad, and maybe it was best to simply believe her, since it was possible that she was in a position to know. Her father had probably been a real shit. Then again, her kids were assholes. But then again, they were just kids. Then again and again.

"Really wonderful out here," his father said as they overlooked a perfect stream trickling from a rocky outcropping. At this point it was all so much natural wallpaper to Alex, a late nineties screen saver.

"It's nice to be somewhere you can think," Alex said. They were competing for a place in the World Series of banality. Dad Sox versus the Alexander Cardinals. Dad in five.

"Don't want too much of that!" his father said, picking his way closer to the water.

The morning was starting to feel like a commercial for a drug to help you painlessly dispose of your demented father. That was a bad thing to think; it would be terrible, Alex knew, if his parents came down with terminal diseases. Unbearable. But worse, for them, in a way, if *he* did while they were still relatively lucid. It would be best if, somehow, none of them developed degenerative illnesses. He felt guilty for the entire line of thought and sought to ameliorate it.

"How's Ellen?" he said. "How are the girls?"

"You know, everyone's doing pretty good," his father said. He spoke in the slightly higher pitched voice that he used when he was avoiding content. "Lily's soccer team is doing really well, actually. She's actually a pretty good player."

He sounded amazed at this—had there been some suggestion that Lily, and Lily's team, would perform substandardly in their recreational soccer league?

"That's great," Alex said, trudging conversationally forward. "And Ellen's good? Work and everything not too bad?"

"Not too bad, no," his father said. "Up and down, but overall pretty good."

Silence. Mountains.

"Are you still in touch with what's-her-name?" his father said finally. "Lisa?"

"A little bit," Alex said. He and Lisa had dated at Amherst four years ago, then broken up when he moved. "Why are you asking?"

"I liked her," his father said. "You could tell she was a good person. I thought she was really good for you."

Alex felt unexpectedly exposed.

"Don't you think *I'm* a good person?"

"Of course," he said immediately. "What are you talking about?"

"I don't know, it just seemed like you went out of your way to describe her as a good person. Like, I don't know, I *need* a good person in my life, for some reason."

"Don't overanalyze it," his father said. "I liked her. She was a pretty girl and a smart girl and she cared about you. But it seems like you're doing just fine. I'm very proud of you."

But why, now, was he *proud*? *Good, proud.* The words had no meaning. They were stand-ins, maybe, for more complicated feelings his father wouldn't express. Alex wanted to be someone who could communicate, who might be able to formulate his thoughts in such a way that they did not require Talmudic study. He thought, to that end, that he should tell Kate that he loved her, maybe, even if there was no future to the relationship, just so that she could hear him say it. He knew he should tell his father that, too, but he didn't think he would hear it the way he wanted him to, now. He'd hear it as an apology, or an accusation.

"Thanks," Alex said. "You want to turn back soon?"

"Whatever you think," his father said.

That night, they had a long dinner at the expensive restaurant in the old hotel on Higgins, followed by wine at the new wine bar.

"Just so you know, this place is *not*, like, the real

Missoula," Alex said. He was tipsy. His earlier seething ambivalence had been sanded down and he was in the mood to share.

"Seems real enough to me," his father said.

"You choose the Matrix," Alex said.

"Excuse me?"

"Like in *The Matrix*. The guy's eating a fancy steak and he's like, 'I choose the Matrix.'"

"You're very strange," his father said.

"You say that, but, I mean, I'm your son," Alex said. "If I'm strange, you're a big part of it."

"I'm a lot of things, Alexander," his father said lightly. "But I'm *not* strange."

"Well, maybe your, uh, *assiduous* attempts to suppress your strangeness are what did it, then."

His father finished his final inch of wine in a long sip.

"I'd be looking at your mother if I were you," he said. "You're *all* strange. Her, your sister, you. I'm not being critical. I'm fine with it. I'm very proud of you no matter how strange you are."

That old pride again. His father paused and signaled with his empty glass to their waitress, a friend of Alex's, that he urgently needed more wine. Then he leaned back against the padded booth, holding his glass at a tilt as though waiting for it to be filled.

"I mean, I'm glad you're not one of these little pony boys," he continued. "I'll say that much at least. I told you about this, right?"

"I think I would remember that, whatever it is," Alex said.

"No? I took Lily to an author signing because she's very into the My Little Pony books right now. *They're back*, apparently, the ponies. And, really she's into the dolls, and the show, not the books, but whatever. We get her the books, it gets her reading. It's all good. *Anyway*, we're at the bookstore, waiting in line, and there are all these guys, boys—I mean, *men*, really—your age, some of them, some older, even, a *lot* older—dressed up as the My Little Ponies. With these pink *tails* coming out of their pants, and pink hair, the whole thing. And I mean, I don't know, I'm saying to Lily, like, Are you *seeing* this? I'm a little bit *skeptical*, let's say. And Lily of course is totally unfazed. She's like, 'They're being *ponies*, Tom. It's a whole thing.' And I'm thinking *Oh-kay*. And, like, how must *that* guy's parents feel? So anyway, I don't care that you're strange. You're barely strange, Alex. I'm just teasing you. But *since* you're not a pony boy, as far as I know, I'm glad you're not. That's all I'm saying."

"There's a lot you don't know," Alex said.

Casey finally came and filled Tom's glass.

"Thank you, dear," his father said abstractedly. He sipped, frowned, and leaned forward.

"There are things a father doesn't need to know," he said. "But you might be surprised by how unsurprised I would be."

This did not have the force of revelation, but that was all right. He didn't want to confess anything to his father. Instead, he grinned across the table at him like a monkey.

"What?" his father said. "*Are* you a pony boy?"

"Maybe," he said. "You know that it's, like, fairly

prevalent in the world, right? Like, that's actually really normal. People do all kinds of things."

"Worse?"

"What would be the worst thing to you?" Alex said. "Like, what would you really not be able to handle?"

His father seemed to grow smaller with the shift in tone.

"Alex," he said, leaning forward, "as long as you're happy, and not hurting anyone, I can make my peace with anything."

"Not hurting anyone? That's your rule?"

"You know," his father said, "you can be very passive-aggressive."

Alex's mind had drifted back to Kate. *She* knew from passive-aggressive. When he told her about this later, she would smirk and say, "You're too passive to be passive-aggressive," and he'd accept it.

He could be her pony boy, he thought. He already was, basically. Pony *man*. Maybe that was the right way to describe his orientation. Was a pony man just a horse? No, he remembered. Ponies were not baby horses. The main difference between ponies and horses was their height.

The Boy Vet

IN JULIA'S SECOND YEAR OF medical school, I lost focus. She went off to the hospital and I stayed home with Kiki, our long-legged Border collie mutt. I didn't cook or clean or bring in much money, and my appearance, even in my own generous self-conception, had declined in recent months from "cover of *Infidels* Dylan" to "sweating and confused at the end of Live Aid Dylan." But the dog made me feel okay about things. She forgave my negligence of her grooming and exercise, and repaid my shoddy fathering with wild delight every time I survived a trip to the bathroom. I counted each hour she stayed alive as a major achievement, a line on my karmic CV.

My *actual* CV was a different story. I'd dropped out of a Ph.D. program in English literature after only a year, feeling, inaccurately, that my brilliance could not be contained by the tedious expectations of my peers and professors in New Haven. Julia and I had been flailing away at a long-distance relationship during our respective first years in graduate school, so declaring that my true calling lay as a practitioner of literature rather than a student allowed me to move to Virginia and pester her up close. A nice thing about my life was that I had some money left from when my grandfather died. He'd loved me, for the most part because I'd enjoyed hearing his intimate and unsettling stories, and continued listening long after my sisters refused to countenance them. The money wouldn't last forever, though, as my mother never tired of telling me. Julia would make plenty eventually, if medical school ever ended, and if—big if—I didn't drive her away with my piteous dallying. I was waiting, I guess, for the unforeseen motivating force that would launch me screaming into my thirties. Please stop me if you've heard any of this before.

One morning, I walked Kiki to the vet's office to pick up her summer flea and tick medicine, a task I'd put off until she was covered in fleas and ticks. While I got rung up at the front desk and Kiki pawed desperately at a cage of orphaned kittens, the vet came in from the back. He'd been our point man at the clinic for the almost-year we'd had our pup. He looked about fifteen, with puffy cheeks, blond bangs, and unfixed teeth. His white coat engulfed him like a trainee priest's cassock. It wasn't clear that he knew anything of the veterinary arts, but he was the only male besides me that Kiki didn't growl at, so Julia and I figured he had to have *something* going for him. Mostly, he was the closest vet to our house.

"Hi, Kiki," the boy vet said. "Hi, Kiki's owner."

The gleam in his eye suggested that he knew my name, but was choosing not to use it.

"What's up, Doc?" I said.

"Bad day so far," he said. "A woman brought in a hit-and-run. The dog needs emergency surgery but he's got no tags, and nobody's called to claim ownership."

"So what happens next?" My interest was polite, if not purely academic.

"We don't usually do major procedures without payment or ID," he said.

"So you're going to let it die?"

"We'd rather not."

I clocked him a little more carefully, examining the smirk that seemed to play permanently around the edges of his mouth, especially when it wasn't warranted.

"Have you been telling this story to everyone who comes in?" I said.

"Sure," the boy vet said. "We want someone to save the dog. Any chance it's you?"

Here, here was the curve. For all of my many faults, I am hopelessly susceptible to appeals for help, the more animalcentric, the better. Julia had recycled enough follow-up mail addressed to me from the World Wildlife Fund to replant an old growth forest full of new red pandas.

"How much is the surgery going to cost?" I said.

"Looking like two thousand bucks, give or take."

"Shouldn't you know for sure?"

"Well, the damage could prove to be more, ah, extensive than we assume."

The boy vet was bobbing his head to some invisible tune as he spoke, pulling me in. Kiki was whining to get out of there, but I felt conflicted. On the one hand, I didn't have that kind of money to spare. On the other, I had a credit card with a criminally generous limit, and, given my lack of income, no sense of a budget whatsoever.

"What kind of dog is it?" I said.

"Looks like a corgi mix," he said. "Maybe some kind of terrier or collie in there."

Julia specifically hated corgis. She'd lived next door to a pair of them one summer and still heard phantom yapping late at night.

"Do we have to keep him if I pay for the surgery?"

"Of course not. You can pay for him and then he can go to the shelter. They'll probably wait a couple of weeks before they put him down."

The world, I remembered, was a terrible place.

"Christ, I'll take him," I said. "You knew I was going to do it."

"Yeah, I kind of figured you would," he said, and shook my hand. The smirk was there in force, and it had colonized his face.

I gave the desk nurse my credit card. She took down the number and said they'd call me if the medical expenses went higher, at which point I'd have to decide all over again whether or not to save the dog.

"How do I know you're not just going to make up a number and charge me more money?" I said.

"That would be really despicable," said the boy vet. Then, as if considering it: "Probably illegal. If somebody, like, investigated it."

"Call and tell me how it goes," I said. "Do I still have to pay if it dies?"

"Yes," he said.

I texted Julia: "Have to pay $2K to save dog, not Kiki, got kind of tricked, we might have new dog, love you."

I walked Kiki back to the house. We'd gotten her from a rescue group hawking puppies in front of a Petco the previous September. Julia had been the one crazy for a dog, but I was wary, knowing the bulk of its care would fall to me while she got her education in gore. But puppies are manipulative shits; that's how they stay alive. Kiki—well, proto-Kiki, alias "Buttercup"—fell asleep in my arms in the trash-strewn field behind the Petco, and I no longer had a choice about it. An hour later, and an exorbitant "adoption fee" poorer, the three of us were on the road in a car weighed down with a thirty-six-pound bag of puppy food, two bowls, three leashes, ten toys, and a large metal cage. Excuse me, "crate."

"There's an *animal* in our car," Julia had whispered, trying not to wake her up.

At home, I started on the dishes as a preemptive karma strike. Julia was working long hours, and I'd been, you'll remember, useless, so there were a lot of dishes. My phone rang and I hoped it would be the vet, but, no, it was my friend Kenny, calling to invite us over for dinner later in the week. I gave him a tentative but optimistic yes. Kenny was my best friend in Virginia, a self-employed mechanic-poet who lived half an hour outside of town. He only had a couple of years on me, but he'd already been a touring jazz guitarist, high school janitor, editorial assistant, line cook. Kenny told me he'd only recently reached his ideal state, which was drinking beer on his back porch in an oil-stained T-shirt while bitching about the hunters on his property, and I was grateful to be party to it. Out of pure decency and/or want of company, he'd hooked me up with occasional summer work, pet-sitting and hauling junk away from people's houses. He let me pretend to be a roughneck when I wanted to.

Now, I drank coffee and watched Kiki root around in the backyard. Bring the stick here. Dig a hole there. Race across the fence barking at the dogs in our blessedly forbearing neighbor's yard. Urgent stuff.

A few hours later, the boy vet finally called.

"Did he make it?" I said.

"Well, he's alive," said the vet, rasping like late Eastwood. "He lost a back leg but I think he'll be all right."

This was a win: who could say no to a three-legged dog?

"How much did it cost?"

"I gave you a discount, actually," he said. "My dad and I settled on an even grand. It helped that you were willing to pay more."

"I appreciate it, man," I said. "When can I take him home?"

"We're going to keep him here tonight, but he should be good by tomorrow."

I thanked him again and hung up. I watched Kiki out the window and wondered whether she would get along with her new playmate. She was awfully moody and disobedient. But maybe all she needed was a friend?

I texted Julia: "lets talk when you can. a great dog can

be ours but only if you are OK with it I hope you are love you." She wasn't supposed to get off of her emergency medicine shift until midnight and she was probably pretty busy until then, but I hoped she'd see the text while suturing a gashed anterior crucifixurade or whatever and start turning the idea over in her sleep-deprived brain. I stared at my phone for an hour but she didn't write back. Kiki brought me a pair of Julia's underwear and I put them on the kitchen table with the socks and bras and other underwear she'd found. Then she settled at my feet with a heavy sigh.

When it had been dark for a while, I drove to a shadowy, expensive bar across town to drink with Saul and Liz. They lived in a vacuumed condo with leather sofas and good cable. They worked real jobs—Saul raised money for the university and Liz worked in the front office of the repertory theater—so they deserved their happy hour, and since they invited me to share it, I sort of deserved it, too.

I slunk into the dim light and there, at the bar, was the boy vet, drinking a beer by himself. I didn't see my friends, so I took the seat next to him.

"Out to celebrate new fatherhood?" he said.

"I'm fairly worried Julia's not going to be happy about this," I said.

"Unilateral decision, eh? Been there, done that."

I surveyed the taps and ordered a beer with a full sentence for a name from Elyse the bartender.

"I didn't know you were friends with Cameron," she said.

"Didn't even know that was his name," I said. "I just call him Dr. Dog."

"We don't ID him," Elyse said. "If you can save the little pussums, you can drink at Red's."

"I'm twenty-three," he said.

"Good for you," I said.

"I actually only graduated from veterinary school a year ago. But my parents've owned the animal hospital my whole life. I was basically born in that stinking place."

"You must get along with your parents pretty well."

He examined the top liquor shelf with what appeared to be despair.

"We . . . collaborate."

I wanted to keep going, but Liz and Saul came down the steps into the bar.

"Do you guys know Cameron?" I said. "The veterinarian?"

"Oh, we've met," Liz said. "We go back."

"Ha," said Cameron. "What up, Liz?"

Saul turned away.

"We're going to get a table," I said. "I'll call you tomorrow about the dog."

"Better yet, I'll call you," he said in a deep, cartoony voice.

We sat down in the back corner of the room, as far from the vet as possible.

"That guy's the creepiest bastard in this town," Saul said.

"He seems okay," I said.

"No, Saul's right," Liz said. "He dated my friend Margot for a while. He was really nasty and possessive, and meanwhile he was cheating on her the whole time with *her* friend Lacey. He was feeding Margot all this insane garbage about how she was a damaged soul, and incapable of real love and whatever, and he'd somehow convinced her that he was some kind of charismatic intellectual or something. He's *troubled*, dude."

"Funny, Liz, how you're leaving an important person out of this story," Saul said.

"Okay, and when I first moved to town I had a very, *very* brief thing with him, too," Liz said. "Until I realized—*very* quickly—what a creep he was. Probably around the time he tried to have sex with me, like, *in the immediate vicinity of his father's grave*."

"Yikes," I said. "He's kind of young for you, no?"

"He's, like, thirty? That's a normal age."

"He just told me he was twenty-three. And that his father still runs the animal hospital."

"Well, he was definitely insisting that we were visiting his father's gravestone, and that he needed to be *comforted*," Liz said. "He was certainly crying enough about it. I guess it's even more awful if it wasn't true."

"He convinced me to adopt an injured dog today," I said. "Will you guys take him if Julia doesn't want him?"

"Allergies, bro," Saul said. "Maybe now that she's a doctor, or almost a doctor, she'll take pity? Like on a medical level?"

"If I were you, I'd bail now," Liz said. "Just like, nip that bud."

"I already paid a thousand dollars for his surgery," I said.

"So you've done your part," Liz said. "Pass the baton. Nobody wins a relay race by himself."

"But I *want* him," I said.

"Don't be a child," Saul said. "That's what I've been telling myself when I want things I shouldn't have, like other women."

"God, please, *have* another woman," Liz said.

When they left after another drink, the boy vet was still at the bar. I took the seat next to him again.

"See that guy down there?" Cameron said. "Doesn't he look like a fatter, balder Tony Romo?"

"Listen," I said. "How old are you really?"

He hunched his shoulders and looked down into his beer.

"I'm thirty-three," he said. "Like Jesus. Nobody ever believes me."

"It makes you seem like you're hiding something."

"Like my age?"

"It also seems like you've dated every woman in town."

"Heh, *dated*," he said. "It can seem that way when they get to talking."

His voice was thick, and he rocked steadily on his stool—*thunk, thunk-thunk*. My phone buzzed. It was a text from Julia: "I know you want another dog and I understand that its important to you I dont want to seem like a jerk not letting you but I really dont think we have space or money for another dog im sorry. Be home after midnight."

"She really doesn't want the dog," I said.

"Aw, tie a fucking bow around its neck. Call it an early Hanukkah present."

"I've been hearing you're not so nice to your girlfriends," I said.

"The fate of old-fashioned men in a world dominated by females."

I took a big gulp of my beer and processed that.

"Now that the corgi's fixed up, don't you think you'll be able to find someone to take him?" I said.

"I guess so, dude. At this point it's more about the principle of the thing, don't you think?"

"Your father teach you that?"

"No, he just made me hateful and dependent. At least I'll inherit the practice when he dies."

I paused, gave him a chance to correct the record, or whatever it was, then let it go.

"It's not going to be worth much if you alienate all your clients," I said.

"I'm a good vet. Say what you want about my quote unquote character. I bring little creatures back to life. And they know I'm good at it, too. Your goddamn dog nearly bit my assistant's hand off, and she's the nicest person I know. But she'll never be a vet. The dogs know she's a hack."

I wasn't quite convinced by this. But it was past ten o'clock and I hadn't had dinner, or fed Kiki. This didn't bode well for the I'm-responsible-enough-to-take-care-of-two-dogs argument I was planning to make. I put some money down on the bar.

"Look, if you want the dog, tell your girlfriend he's old and probably won't last much longer," he said.

"Is that true?"

"As far as you know."

It was that ancient, nasty confidence. I could see how

he convinced people to sleep with him. I could also see him getting stabbed between the ribs.

When I pulled up to the house, Kiki bolted from the bushes across the street and met the car on her hind legs, front paws scrabbling the air in greeting.

"What the hell, Keek?" I said. "Can you jump the fence now?"

I walked her to the backyard and saw that the gate was unlatched and hanging open. I tried to work up indignation at the imagined dog-hating passerby who had done this, but fell short. It was on me. I needed to do better.

I brought Kiki inside and poured myself some bourbon. Then I put a frozen pizza in the oven, the kind with vegetables on it, for health. I considered doing something overtly thoughtful for Julia, like buying groceries or cleaning the bathtub, but I decided it was too risky. Once, during a tough month for her, I got up at five in the morning to make pancakes. In my half-awake stupor, I managed to slice my hand open on a nail sticking out of the cabinet. She ended up at the hospital half an hour before her shift and got me sewn up by one of her incompetent classmates. I'd steered clear of caring gestures since.

An hour later, as I was finishing the pizza, I heard Kiki barking like a maniac, which meant that Julia was home.

"It's just Mama," I said, but she didn't quiet down until Julia came through the door, and then jumped up and left muddy paw prints on her scrubs.

Julia took out her earbuds and gave me a kiss.

"You know who's really good?" she said. "DMX. I mean,

obviously. But I just listened to 'Up in Here' like five times on the way home."

"Because you're so angry?" I said.

"I'm better now," Julia said. "Gonna go change, and then we'll talk about this . . . situation."

She emerged from the bedroom a few minutes later wearing a WTJU T-shirt and glasses. She made a pot of tea while I told her about the day.

"I know you just want me to be cool or whatever and say yes, like I'm your mother."

"How is that like my mother?"

"Well, because you're being the kid who wants a puppy, and I'm being the adult who makes the rules."

"It's not a puppy, though," I said. "It's an old dog that probably isn't going to live much longer."

"Great. I can't wait to come home to your dead dog."

"*Our* dead dog," I said.

The teakettle whistled and she poured herself a cup. I retaliated by pouring more bourbon into my half-full drink.

"Look, I'm willing to go see it. Which, by the way, you haven't done yet. What if it's awful? What if it's disgusting?"

"That's fair," I said. "Let's do that. And if it's a bad dog, maybe it *deserves* to die."

"I didn't say that."

I called and left a message at Cameron's office, said we'd be by around 4:30, when Julia's shift was over. Then I went to the couch and put my head in Julia's lap.

"Ken invited us over for Thursday night," I said. "Wouldn't it be great to just show up with a new dog?"

"The little guy'd probably make a run for it when the yelling and puking started," she said.

"Dogs love those things," I said.

My phone buzzed.

"I should get this."

Julia went off down the hall with Kiki at her heels.

"So you're not taking the dog," the boy vet said. Or something like that—I could barely understand him through the slur in his voice.

"We're going to visit and decide together," I said.

"Dragged in by the tip of your dick," he said. A chorus of barks rose in the background.

"Are you at the clinic?"

"It's *more* than a job, *man*. I was keeping your crippled pooch company so it wouldn't up and die on me. But now I'm thinking I might as well save him the despair of dashed hopes."

"Um," I said.

"It's bye-bye for the little bow-wow," he said. He made his voice hoarse and lugubrious. "Nobody loves you, bow-wow."

"You're not helping your cause."

"Bedtime for the bow-wow. 'Bye now, bow-wow. Bye-bye."

He started howling into the phone, and then abruptly hung up. Seconds later, his number flashed on my phone again. I let it vibrate on the coffee table until "Missed Call" flashed on the screen. This happened twice more before I turned my phone off.

"Why was he calling now?" Julia said. Kiki jumped

from my spot and pulled herself under the bed, back claws splayed and skittering behind her.

"Guess he works late," I said.

I got into bed next to Julia, who was still wearing her T-shirt, and, it transpired, nothing else.

"Do you ever worry that I care too much about Kiki and don't give you enough attention?" I said.

"No," Julia said. "I have real things to worry about."

Kiki crunched on something under the bed, probably a pen or a phone charger.

"Kiss me," I said. When she leaned in, I pressed my hand to her forehead and held her back.

"Come on, kiss me," I said. She pushed against my hand.

"Do you like that?" I said.

"Not particularly," she said.

When the appointed hour arrived the next day, I met Julia, with Kiki in tow, in the parking lot of the vet's office. The nurse at the front desk didn't have any idea what we were talking about.

"Is Doctor . . . is doctor even the right word? Is Cameron in?" I said.

"Oh, he's back there someplace," the nurse said. "He's not so talkative today."

We sat in the waiting room for twenty minutes. Finally, he emerged from the back, eyes bloodshot, with a loosened Goofy tie visible under his open white coat.

"Sonny and Cher," he said when he saw us. "How's that good girl of yours?"

"Kiki's fine," I said.

"Excellent, excellent," he said. "What can I help you with?"

"We're here to see the corgi. The one whose surgery I paid for."

"Oh. Right," he said solemnly. He pinched the bridge of his nose. "Right."

"What is it?" Julia said.

"That dog . . . well, he took a big chunk out of a volunteer this morning. Attacked her. She needed fifteen stitches, actually."

"Oh my God," Julia said.

"We had to put him down," the vet said. "I'm so sorry to have to tell you. I guess you're lucky it wasn't you that got bit, though. You know?"

"Is this true?" I asked the desk nurse. "Did this girl get mauled? By a *corgi*?"

"*I* just got here," the nurse said. "Nobody tells me about anything."

"There's really no way to know, is there?" I said. I had a dim but rising fear that I'd hallucinated the past twenty-four hours.

"You want to see him?" the vet said. "He's still in the back. I mean, his body is."

"I think we're fine," Julia said.

"I do," I said. Misplaced kindness had gotten me into this, and now morbid curiosity was going to see me through to the end.

"Come on, then." We walked back into a consultation room and he closed the door behind him. On the wall there was a framed photograph of baby Cameron holding hands with a diapered chimpanzee.

"You think we just keep dead dogs lying around here?" he said hurriedly. "Grow up, man. You wouldn't have been able to keep it anyway."

"What did you do?"

"I refunded you the cost of the surgery," he said. "So you don't have to worry about your *credit card bill*." He said it like it was some made-up thing that he was only acknowledging to humor me.

"And you murdered the dog?"

"I'm not saying that. Look, the whole thing's been pretty complicated, man. It just wasn't meant to be."

He leaned unsteadily against the rolling metal examination table for support and let out a big, sick-sounding breath.

"I heard that your father died," I said.

"Yeah, I heard that, too," he said. "Must be something going around." He put his head down on the table and rolled it forward a few inches, then pulled it back. My own father would have called this "thrashing"; it meant a nap was in order. I stood there in silence.

"I'm sure there's a dead animal back here somewhere," he said. "Or will be soon enough."

Julia told me the other night that, after years of meditating, she'd decided that Buddhism was mostly just about being nice to people. I hadn't joined her on her Zen kick, but it was a useful idea to fall back on when the alternative was imminent assault.

"There was a dog in all this, at some point, right?" I said.

He brushed his hair out of his eyes and raised his head. "Don't you have any kind of an imagination?" he said.

In this moment, in this desperate light, he looked his age—that is, my age—if not significantly older. Whatever was inside him, whatever was driving this, was taking a heavier toll on him than it would on me. Or so I hoped.

I let him lead me back out to the waiting room. Julia was reading a pamphlet on heartworm and Kiki was curled up tight under her chair, staring at me from under her beautiful eyelashes.

"I'll let you know the next time we have a good candidate for you." He shook my hand and, I swear, winked at me, before walking back toward his office. Kiki stood up and gnawed on my wrist. *Ready to go, Dad.* We all got into Julia's Mini and drove in silence.

"Was it awful?" Julia said. "Seeing the dog?"

Out the window, I watched a road crew worker scratch his back with an orange SLOW sign.

"It just looked like it was sleeping," I said.

A couple of evenings later, I drove out through the hills of horse country to Kenny's house with Kiki sprawled in the backseat. Julia was back home overstudying for yet another standardized test, mostly, I think, to get out of coming along for the visit. I watched the stretches of dense forest open onto lit-up fields. Kenny and Scruggs, his vicious Jack Russell, were waiting at the end of his winding driveway, standing alongside Kenny's truck and an old Volkswagen. Kiki bolted through a lowered car-window at Scruggs, who immediately dropped into a sprint across the meadow in front of the house. From a copse of bushes, a corgi burst into the field and chased desperately and ineffectually after them.

"New dog?" I said.

"Nah, that's Cam's pup," he said. "He's just over for a bit with his wife. Guy's insane but mostly all right."

"Jesus," I said. But how else could this story end?

There was Cameron, posted up in the kitchen in a flowered apron, frying a mess of hamburger meat on the stove and drinking from a bottle of George Dickel. His supposed wife was leaning back against the sink in jeans and a frayed Widespread Panic T-shirt. She had a short shock of gray hair. She smiled thinly at me and waved like she had an invisible cigarette between her fingers. Cameron turned to me, unsurprised.

"Brought you a dog," he said. "Made him alive and put all his legs back on for you, too."

The woman swatted at his head and whacked him pretty hard, to no discernible effect.

"Actually, you *can't* have Popcorn," she said. "He's ours, no matter how many times Cam tries to give him away."

I just stared at her.

"We get that a lot," she said, nodding. "It's a really normal reaction. Nora." She reached out her hand and I shook it wearily.

"You looking for a dog?" Kenny said. "Take Scruggsy here. He'll make good eatin'."

The dogs had assembled in the living room, drawn by

the smell of the cooking meat. They were lined up, one, two, three, like animated chipmunks on a windowsill. Kiki scratched furiously at her collar, at a dead tick, maybe, buried in her neck.

"Cameron's been having problems with his medication," Nora said. "There's no way he can keep going in to work like this. We've lost, like, five regulars this week. Not *lost* lost. Just, you know, people who are never coming back. Which is fair. I mean, *I* wouldn't."

Kenny handed me a beer and I took a pull from it as I contemplated this. Cameron's gaze was concentrated on the pan in front of him. He mushed the meat flat until it smoked.

"Trust her, man," Cameron mumbled. "It'll be better if you trust her."

"Trust me!" Nora said. "Trust me, trust me!"

I didn't trust them, though Cameron now seemed barely conscious enough to qualify as a person, let alone an antagonist. My helpless sympathy extended itself to him, to all of us.

"That burger looks just about done, Cam," Kenny said. It was quite badly charred. *"I've got a few I cooked earlier keeping warm in the oven,"* he stage-whispered to me.

I helped carry the food outside to a battered picnic table, feeling dazed by my empty-stomach beer and the lowering twilight and the company I was keeping. We chewed burgers and watched the dogs chase each other in circles. I drank another beer.

"I think, probably, I need a new *task*," Cameron said suddenly. "Something to concentrate my energy on so that I can bring positivity into the world instead of all this nightmare stuff."

"Here's one," Kenny said. "Finish your drink."

"You shouldn't be drinking," Nora said quietly, and dumped Cameron's glass of whiskey onto the lawn. "I'm an influence," she said to the table.

As it got dark we made a fire with some of the old furniture that was scattered around the backyard. We threw a tennis ball to the dogs, but Scruggs was the one who brought it back every time, Kiki nipping at his heels, Popcorn just giving up and lying in wait to ambush them on their return trip. I sipped whiskey out of the bottle and stared into the fire as Kenny told stories about the time he broke up a fight at Malone's, the time he started a fight at the 2:19, the time, the time . . .

Cameron fell asleep with his head in Nora's lap. She laughed in the right places as Kenny told stories, but it seemed to me that her mind was on her boy vet. She stroked his hair with tender repetition and maintained an expression of wonder no matter how grotesque the behavior Kenny recounted. I didn't think she and Cameron were actually married, but it did seem like she loved him, and maybe, in his way, he loved her, too. I felt a tug of jealousy for their mutual madness, or whatever it was.

"Happy," I said to Nora. I'd meant it as a question to her.

"Good," she said.

In an increasingly rare stretch of lucidity, I realized, staring into the fire, that it had been a long time since I'd seen my dog, so I got up and walked toward the trees calling her name. Scruggs emerged with the ball gripped in his teeth.

"Where's your friend?" I said. "Where's Kiki?"

He ran back into the woods, as if he were really going to go find her for me, and I watched his small white body disappear into the darkness. I listened hard for the jingle of dog tags. Nothing.

"She'll come back," Kenny said. I hadn't realized he was beside me.

"What if she chased after a deer and got lost?" I said. "What if she's stuck in barbed wire somewhere?"

"Well, then I guess you fucked up," said Kenny.

We sat by the fire a while longer, letting it burn down to a low smolder. The special guest couple went to bed, Cameron trailing after Nora like a sleepy child up the dark path to the house. Kenny and I followed after them and listened to Roy Orbison on the turntable for a while. Scruggs curled up on my lap and I rubbed his head, listening for any sign of Kiki's return.

"I've got to find my dog," I said. "*Shit.* I'm gonna walk around a little and see what I can see."

I was too drunk to be doing this, and I wanted Ken to tell me not to bother, but he just said, "Besta luck," and knelt down to find a new record. I went out the back door and into the woods, calling out her name and clapping. I heard my claps echoing back at me, sure, but when those faded I heard, or willed myself to hear, a faint howling in the distance. I walked in that direction, and immediately lost any sense of where I was.

I must have wandered a while in the darkness, clapping and calling—I have no idea how long or far I went—but I do have a clear image of Kiki emerging from the bank of a pond, soaked to her essential skinniness, grinning. *Oh, my fucking dog*, I thought. *My life.*

I bent and picked her up, all fifty pounds of her, and hugged her to my chest as she squirmed and tried to jump away. I didn't know where the house was, obviously. My arms were already aching with the weight of the dog and my shirt was soaked through, but I wasn't about to put her back down. I paused, hoping for some kind of sign, some hint of recognition as to the right way to go, but it wasn't forthcoming. I picked a direction and walked.

Deep Cut

"NAW, YOU DON'T HAVE TO worry about me," Thomas said, after his mother had finished her characteristically perfunctory warning to us about drugs, alcohol, and rough-looking types. "*Paul* thinks he's cool now, though."

"Paul, when did this happen?" Mrs. Rickley said.

She wasn't a hip mom, exactly, but she got points for not caring particularly about what her children or their friends got up to. She was a physics professor at Princeton and had consistently made it clear that she did not need this shit.

"I just woke up one morning wearing Ray-Bans," I said. "I guess it was for an album cover shoot, and it kind of spiraled out from there."

"He's trying to impress girls now," Thomas said.

"Oh, God forbid, Thomas," his mom said. "Maybe *you* should try to impress a girl. After your hair grows back. And don't be a smart-ass, Paul."

Thomas had surprised me with a freshly Bic'd skull and

a three-piece suit when I arrived at his house a few hours before the concert. His light blond hair and pale skin had already rendered him a solid candidate for the Hitler Youth; now he looked like genuine trouble, or at least troubled. The new look was an homage to one of the bands we were going to see, Execution of Babyface, each of whose members rocked the "shaved head/natty threads" combo. The EOB fans were notoriously violent, even for hardcore kids, and Thomas and I, best friends and cultural comrades since we were ten years old, had spent a lot of time on message boards reading—probably?—untrue rumors about coordinated windmill fist phalanxes and secret seven-inches given only to "executioners" who could present the band with a tooth, or teeth, knocked free during a show. It was all a bit scary and conspiratorial for punk rock, and, even at that early stage, it was much more Thomas's scene than mine. But I did enjoy the music, or was at least fascinated by it. It was pulverizing and ultra-fast and punctuated by terrifying screams. EOB's lyrics were inspired by Guy Debord, Ashbery poems, and Kevin Smith movies, though you generally couldn't catch them in real time. It was a substantial leap from the Punk 101 I'd absorbed from a rudimentary website run by a Russian autodidact, which was filled with long paeans to the brilliance of *London Calling*, *Zen Arcade*, and the brief, collected works of Rites of Spring. I'd just turned sixteen.

Mrs. Rickley pulled up to the venue, which turned out to be a wide single-story building off of Route 35, a quiet highway in South Amboy, wherever that was. Before I learned to drive, I never had any idea of my location in space—it seemed impossible to pay attention to something like that from a backseat, and so I never tried. There were only a couple of years between my learning to drive and the rise of the talking navigation machines, which reduced the world to their glowing screens and precise, incorrectly pronounced instructions. In other words: Is it any wonder I still have no idea where I am?

"All right, guys, I'll be back for you at midnight," Mrs. Rickley said. "Be ready. For every minute you're late I'm going to—what? Dock your allowance? Do you *have* an allowance?"

"Sure, we'll come out when the show's over," Thomas said.

"I know *Paul* heard what I said," she said.

"Yeah, we'll definitely meet you out here when the show's finished," I said.

"Paul, do *not* be an asshole to me. I'll see you here at twelve."

She drove off and we walked the length of a long line of people waiting to get inside. It looked to be maybe one-third EOB guys—all *guys*—trying not to look self-conscious in their suits, one-third old-school punks in the usual leather, plaid bondage pants, and assorted paraphernalia, and one-third shaggy-haired emo-adjacent kids in black T-shirts and jeans, like me. We finally found the end of the line, wrapped all the way around the back of the building.

"Doors were at seven and it's eight-fifteen, so I sure fucking hope we're not missing Class of '36," Thomas said.

"It shouldn't be that hard to get people in," I said.

A raccoon-eyed girl in a leather jacket turned around.

"Some EOB jackass threw a smoke bomb before anyone even went on," she said. "So everybody had to leave and come back in. And now they're doing, like, cavity searches, I guess."

"Fucking fascists," Thomas said, though the security response sounded reasonable enough to me. He took a Swiss Army knife out of the breast pocket of his suit jacket and contemplated it.

"Why did you bring that?" I said.

"Open stuff," he mumbled. He crouched down next to a shrub on the side of the building and clawed at the mulch below, then dropped his knife in the hole and covered it back up.

"Like fifty people just watched you do that," I said.

"Punk is trust," he said.

We inched forward. I wished I had a cigarette—wished I *smoked* cigarettes. This was what they had been designed for, looking cool while waiting for things. Word was you could buy them, no questions asked, at the kiosk in Palmer Square as long as you were sure that no one from school was around. Though he'd never said it, my guess was that cigarettes were even lower in Thomas's moral hierarchy than alcohol or drugs or sex because the pose-to-effect ratio was so high. Per Minor Threat: *I. JUST. THOUGHT. IT. LOOKED COOL.*

Thomas shadowboxed next to me.

"What, is, the, *holdup*?" he said, punctuating the last word with a knockout punch.

"Class of '36 kind of sucks anyway," I said. They were, again per the Internet, third-tier Rancid knockoffs, with lots of "oi oi ois" and rousing shit about the Spanish Civil War.

"They're better than standing around looking at a closed fucking *auto parts* shop," Thomas said.

A couple of minutes later, a chant went up in the crowd: "EOB. LET US IN. EOB. TEAR IT DOWN. EOB. FUCK YOUR LIFE." Despite the infamy of the band, and the implied threat of their chanted lyrics, this didn't strike me as a crowd that was going to start a riot, at least not right away. But the recitation gained force, and, sudden as the opening of a traffic bottleneck when the wrecked car is finally towed, we were moving swiftly toward the door.

"*Finally*, collective *action*," said the mohawked guy ahead of us. He dropped his cigarette and pulverized it into a smear of tobacco with a heavy black boot.

"All right, dude," Thomas said. "Things might get crazy in there, so we've gotta have each other's backs. If we see one of us getting in trouble, we're gonna step up, right?"

"Don't do something stupid," I said. "You're not that big."

"I'm here to go all-out, man."

The old anxiety bubbled in me, less fear than anticipation. I wanted, then, and always, to have the best night of my life, to do whatever thing would change me forever. Everything I read and listened to insisted that all was building toward catharsis. There could be no complete self without eruption, revelation, and the possibility of total defeat, however unlikely.

At the door, the fat white bouncer gave me a cursory pat-down—pockets, belly, chest, go—but he held Thomas back and made him take off his jacket and vest, lift up his shirt, even stick out his tongue.

"Profiling sons of bitches," he muttered.

"'*Scuse* me, son?" the bouncer said.

"You're doing a very good and thorough job," Thomas said.

At the ID table, I received the black *X*'s in Sharpie on the backs of my hands. Thomas had apparently already drawn red ones on his, a frequent enough occurrence, I guess, that the ID guy simply waved him on, eye roll very much implied.

Class of '36 was in the middle of a song when we got into the main room, the one with the chorus that went "*Whoa-ah-uh-uh-oh, we're taking it!*" Maybe fifty people were jumping in place or standing with their arms crossed in front of the stage, occasionally shoving the skinny kids who were doing the stumbling-and-swaying-while-being-overcome-with-feeling thing. Save it for your subgenre, guys. Most of the EOB and hardcore-looking guys were stalking around away from the stage, looming over the merch table, wandering along the walls giving fist bumps to confederates. The bar was being used as a convenient leaning post by large, bearded dudes in hooded sweatshirts, most of whom were drinking water out of clear plastic cups, if anything. Over the course of the night, I saw people swigging out of flasks and label-less plastic bottles and discreetly hitting one-hitters, but I didn't see a single person buy a drink at the bar.

The merch table had a copy of the original *Babyface* EP on vinyl, which came out before the band was forced to change its name because of a cease-and-desist order from Arista Records. (As if consumers would somehow mistake a violent, surrealist hardcore band for the smooth-singing R&B guy, but whatever.) I wanted to buy it, but didn't know what I'd do with it during the show.

"How many of those do you have?" I shouted.

"Extremely limited, dude," the merch guy shouted back. He was good at his job.

I sighed and bought it for ten bucks, put it under my arm, went looking for Thomas. I spotted him near the wall to the left of the stage, glaring furiously at the band.

"You were right, they fucking suck," Thomas said.

"They're actually better than I thought they'd be," I said. I did think that, but I mostly wanted to contradict him.

He turned his attention to me. "I already have that," he said, nodding at the record.

"You never see it around, so I figured I should grab it," I said.

"Right, because rarity is an accurate proxy for significance."

"I'm with capitalism on that one, yeah."

Thomas turned his attention back to the stage. "It's gonna get all fucked up in the pit."

I put the record on the floor, leaning it against the wall, my carelessness intended as a further misguided rebuke to Thomas, and walked away into the thickening crowd.

"I want to thank all you motherfuckers for keeping it real and keeping real punk the fuck alive," the lead singer of Class of '36 said. "This is our last song, it's about not giving a fuck whether you live or die. Everybody stay safe tonight, look out for each other."

They started into "Suicide Mission," and people surged forward, shoving and skanking and, in a few cases, wildly swinging their fists. A skinny guy with a buzz cut caught my eye and gave me a frantic, bobbing thumbs-up. I gave him one back.

"*Up, up!*" he shouted. He lifted one foot off the ground and pressed his hand into my shoulder. I didn't understand that he wanted to crowd-surf until he tried to plant his foot in the middle of my leg, at which point I bent down and let him use my thigh for leverage. He stomped down on me and dug his fingers deeper into my shoulder and remained poised in that precarious state until a girl in a tank top crouched under his other foot and hoisted him up onto the heads of the people in front of us, who put their arms up and passed him forward. The guy lay on his back, aloft, and pumped his fist slightly out of time with the lyrics of the chorus:

"I said *CHELSEA*, I'm not coming back, the smoke is coming in and we're under attack. It's a *SUICIDE MISSION*, there's no turning back, the flames are getting high and the walls are turning black . . ."

A girl rocking tattoo sleeves with a flowered sundress clambered up on the stage, saluted the audience, then went stiff and fell face-first into the pit. She was caught and passed back through the crowd. A pair of hands egregiously grabbed her breasts, prompting her to kick her heavy boots—hard—at the heads of the people holding her legs, which caused the bottom half of her body to abruptly drop to the floor. Somebody—quite possibly the guy who'd groped her in the first place—lifted her up by the armpits and stood her upright, at which point she immediately resumed head-banging and charged back toward the stage.

When the band finished, the PA played "Search and Destroy" at half the volume of the live set and people drifted toward the edges of the room. I spotted Thomas sitting against the wall in the spot where I'd left him. He had his hands to his temples and he was staring at his lap. Oh, was the lame-ass opening band too loud for him? There were still two more to go before the band he wanted to see.

I left him alone and drifted out a side door to the smoking area, a small concrete patio enclosed by a genuine red velvet rope. Most of the smokers looked much older than me, but a round-faced girl with pink streaks in her hair looked open to solicitation.

"Nice to see a Cure shirt in the mix," I said.

"Wanted to remind the emo kids," she said. "Boys, just *don't.*"

"Word," I said. Under my hoodie, I was wearing the Get Up Kids T-shirt with the brass knuckles on it, which was funny, in theory, because the Get Up Kids were extremely sensitive. "I know this is awful, but is there any chance I could trouble you for a cigarette?"

"Sigh," she said. "Start 'em young, I guess."

She offered me a cigarette and a lighter. It was a Parliament, and I turned it end over end a couple of times to make sure I didn't light the filter. Then I flicked the lighter repeatedly, failing to create a flame. I shook it and cupped my hand around it and tried again. Nothing.

"Windy," I said, though it wasn't.

"Here," she said, and took the lighter. I put the cigarette in my mouth and she held the fire to it.

"Inhale, man, inhale!" she said. I did, and started coughing when the smoke hit my lungs.

"Oh man, you do *not* smoke," she said.

"I just haven't in a while," I said.

"It's okay, dude. Gotta start somewhere. Who are you here to see?"

"My buddy's super into EOB. I don't know the other bands that much."

"Oh, Fall to Shadows is next. They're all right, but if you're into more melodic stuff, I think you'll dig Secret Keepers. They're on second-to-last. I can see that Get Up Kids shirt peeking out there, no worries."

"You are one on whom nothing is lost," I said. I'd read about Henry James recently because a girl I thought I liked had told me that *The Portrait of a Lady* was her favorite novel. I'd taken *The Golden Bowl* out of the library, but it might as well have been in German for all the sense I could make of it.

"Fuck, yeah, dude," she said. "And I'm Karen, thanks for asking. Kind of a scene queen."

"Paul," I said. "Straight-up wannabe."

"It's a glamorous life, for sure."

The cigarette was going down easier now, though it still felt pretty terrible, and was making me light-headed.

"Is this Babyface stuff really as nuts as everyone says it is?" I said.

"I mean, it's definitely *violent*," Karen said. "As a putative member of the fairer sex, I prefer not to get in the middle of it, but it's not much worse than the usual dumb hardcore shit. Unless you piss off one of the idiots. You shouldn't wear your glasses."

"I'm pretty blind without them."

"Exactly. You wanna go in?"

She flicked her lit cigarette an impressive distance into the street. I dropped mine on the ground and put it out with my heel, then picked it up and tossed it underhand over the velvet rope.

"Aw, newbie," Karen said.

"How old are *you*?" I said.

"Sixteen. Well, in a couple months. See you inside."

I waited a polite ten seconds and then followed her. A big crowd was gathered for the next band, and I didn't see Thomas among them, or against the wall. My record was still there, though, looking intact. Maybe punk *was* trust. *Raw Power* had gotten to "I Need Somebody," which meant that a band had to be coming on soon; surely it was bad form to let an entire *album* play between sets? I saw the guy who'd crowd-surfed off of me and he gave me a curt nod. Then the lights went down and the crowd pushed forward. I let the people go around me and stood in front of the line of burly, self-appointed enforcers. When I looked over my shoulder, I saw that Thomas was among them, almost right behind me, arms crossed, feet set.

"I thought you'd abandoned me," I said.

"Naw, man, that nostalgic shit just gives me a headache," he said. "I'm straight now, though. Smoking is bad for you."

"Yeah, it makes you feel like shit, too," I said.

Thomas looked highly energized, so much that I was almost suspicious. Surely he hadn't . . . *done* anything, substance-wise? There was no way to ask without pissing him off, and I liked him better like this, whatever the cause. We watched the set from a defensive position in the back of the scrum, shoving flailing kids back into the pit and helping fallen girls and large men alike off of the increasingly slippery floor. Fall to Shadows weren't bad, despite their unfortunate nu-metal vibe and the fact that I wasn't at all sure what they were on about. ("I lament (?) you from my—[shaking? shaven?]—chest [____], WAHHHHHHHHHHHHHHHH!") When they finished, we ambled to the bar like victorious athletes and gulped water.

Thomas spent the keyboard-heavy, sparsely attended Secret Keepers set bobbing on his toes and opening and closing his fists while I bopped along, too, semi-bored. Seconds after they finished—"You guys are fucking awesome, EOB is up next, everybody be safe out there"—the men in suits started pressing forward, pushing us up to the front of the stage.

"Are you cool with this?" Thomas said.

"We're here, right?" I said.

We were surrounded by pinstripes and solemn, shiny heads. Some of the suit jackets had been decked out with punk stuff—metal studs, anarchy-symbol pocket handkerchiefs—but most were anonymous, which, as intended, just made them more intimidating. A roadie in a suit came onstage.

"CHECKKKKKKKKKKKK!" he screamed, neck

veins bulging. He pointed upward. Louder. "CHECK-CHECKCHECK CHECKKKKKKKKKKKKKK." He pointed upward again. "CHECK MOTHERFUCKING CHECK," he screamed. "CHECK DIEEEEEEEEEEEEEE DIE DIE." This got big cheers.

Then, without further warning, the band was onstage, hurriedly plugging cords into guitars. We were right up against the metal barrier in front of the stage, and I felt hands pressing into my back and shoulders, urging me to create space where there was none.

"All right, motherfuckers, you know who the fuck we are," the lead singer said. "We don't want nobody getting killed tonight. But if there's, uh, a little damage along the way, who's to say we won't be a little stronger for it? This is 'Variation on a Spectacle,' let's go."

The band crashed into the song with double-time drums and chest-shaking bass and some unpredictable, processed shrieks that must have been emanating from a guitar. The room disappeared into darkness interrupted by toxic green strobe flashes. Thomas spun away from me and into the pit. Someone to my right gave me a hard shove in the lower back and I stumbled toward the melee of thrashing people. I kept my hands in front of me and hip-checked a skinny kid into the open floor. *Hell* yes. For about five seconds, I felt the pure exhilaration promised by a thousand Greil Marcus columns. Then I turned and caught an elbow in the face, the pain so blunt and clarifying that it didn't register as pain, pure heat without humidity. My glasses went flying and my vision was reduced to glowing red spots underlaid by a sick green. When the music paused, because all of EOB's songs were about ninety seconds long, I heard a crack, followed by the fatal crunch of lens underfoot.

"Glasses!" I called out. "Anybody see glasses?"

A blurry someone handed me some bent plastic.

"They're pretty fucked, bro," he said. "And your face's bleeding."

Somebody grabbed my shoulder. Thomas, blurry.

"Who did this?" he shouted.

"Nobody," I said. "It was just random."

"Nothing is random, dude," he said.

The music returned, faster and louder than before, and I ducked behind the sweatshirt mafia. I touched my finger to my eyebrow and it came away wet. Not great. I held the broken glasses up to my face. One of the lenses was still intact, so I pressed it to my eye socket and moved back toward the main thrashing mass, trying to fulfill my pledge to keep an eye—if *only* an eye—cute, buddy—on Thomas. I held my watch an inch from the usable lens. It was ten minutes until midnight.

I watched Thomas, in his ridiculous suit, beautiful and stupid, swinging his arms crazily through the air with great speed and no attempt at coordination. He clocked a large, bald devotee in the nose; the guy stumbled away, then turned and rushed at him, launching into Thomas with a linebacker tackle. Thomas's limbs jerked like a wounded insect's under the guy, who held him down with both hands. I dropped my broken glasses and rushed toward them, hearing, when I got close, the stream of their obscenities through the music. I gave the blurry antagonist a shove, and he didn't move, didn't even seem to acknowledge that I'd touched him, and though I hadn't put everything I had into it, it seemed like an ominous sign. I grabbed blindly at him again, getting ahold of the collar of his jacket, and felt it tear under my hands. Now this indistinct mass of person turned, unlocked himself from Thomas, and stood over me. He shouted something in my direction. I covered my sweat-wet face, trying to shield myself from whatever was going to happen next. I felt his hand on my shoulder, heard more indistinct shouting through the music. Then it clarified:

"Dude, you're fucking bleeding everywhere," the guy said. "I'd beat the shit out of you, if that's what you're into, but you're *covered* in blood."

I held my hands out in front of me—the guy, whatever his other shortcomings, was right about the blood. It seemed to be running freely down my face. The shadowy outline of Thomas had materialized, too, and, though I couldn't see him, I sensed concern.

"Okay, buddy," he said, or something like that, and steered me past the big guys to the bar. I pressed a pile of napkins to my head and held it there. In my mind's eye, I was impressed by my own stoicism, which I guess indicated how detached I was, a result, I supposed, of my lack of sight and the knock to the head and the dehydration and the minor blood loss. It wasn't, Thomas declared, squinting above my eye, a deep cut. I leaned against the bar, letting the music deafen me as he dabbed.

(By the time we started wearing earplugs, in our late twenties, it was too late to turn back the significant hearing loss we'd incurred, Thomas's much worse than mine due to the daily sonic pummeling of the bands that he led during the years I was in college and law school. When Republic of Suffering, his most successful touring concern, came to D.C. during my clerkship year, we stayed up deep into the night in my apartment, catching up. Though by then he'd modified his policy of strict abstinence, Tom probably drank one beer for every three of mine, and I was, and still am, impressed and puzzled by the fact that he hadn't taken to booze or drugs as a default response to life's typical setbacks. At 4:00 a.m. I heard a faint pounding from my front door. It was the guy from the next apartment over, a muscled young political aide with perpetually wet hair. We were, he said, shouting at the top of our lungs. Didn't we know it was four in the morning? He had to be up in an hour. We were sorry. When I spoke to Thomas in a quieter voice, I saw in his eyes the effort required to follow along. His responses grew terse and general, like those of someone responding tentatively to questions in a foreign language, and we soon gave up and went to bed.)

"Do you mind if I get back in there?" Thomas said with a longing glance toward the pit.

"Yeah, no," I said. "I mean, of course. Get me a tooth."

He vanished and my head started to throb, which, at that moment, I found preferable to the alien light-headedness I'd been experiencing. I hadn't quite realized until then that every one of Execution of Babyface's songs was exactly the same. With that revelation came an unlikely surge in desire to join their thick-skulled brotherhood.

"Oof, dude," said a familiar female voice next to me.

"You caused this," I said.

"Aw, let Mama kiss it," Karen said.

I waved her away, though I didn't think she was serious.

"I can't see shit," I said.

"Bald guys playing instruments. Bald guys punching each other. You're not missing much."

"At least the music's good."

"They're a little math-y, don't you think? Not a lot of human stuff."

"The lyrics are actually . . ."

"Yeah, right, I know. But it's kind of a waste, don't you think?"

We let the music hit us.

"It's funny that you can't see," Karen said, very close to my ear. I was worried that she really might kiss me. Then, wetly, nearly inside my head: "You're just some fucking tourist, aren't you?"

I tried to focus on her.

"Maybe," I said. "So?"

"Just giving you shit," she said. "Everybody's a tourist. Except Sid Vicious. Kill Devotion's playing in two weeks at Hamilton Street. Come hang out. Your face is still bleeding."

The maelstrom of noise started up again and she drifted away from me. Up on the edge of the stage, I could just make out something that I assumed was the lead singer of EOB, bent over, screaming.

"And you," he bellowed. "Thank you for your book and yeeeeeeeeeeeeeeear. Something happened in the GARAGE, and I owe it for the BLOOD!"

"Traffic!" the crowd responded.

"Those lines are by the only real American poet," the singer said. "There will be no encore, go home and kill yourselves, good night."

Thomas led me back to the wall to retrieve my record, still standing where I'd left it. I pulled it out of the sleeve. It had broken in two, one chunk significantly larger than the other. I handed the smaller piece to Thomas. We walked outside, and the October air turned our sweat cold immediately. Thomas was shivering but trying not to show it.

"Do you see your mom?" I said. I was no help in spotting her, of course, and was worried that even no-worries Mrs. R would be freaked out by my grisly appearance. It had to be well past midnight.

"Naw," Thomas said, scanning the parking lot.

It turned out we were being taught a lesson about coming out late—since we'd made *her* wait half an hour, she was going to make *us* wait for as long as she deemed fit. Which of course, like most parental punishments, just wasted more of her own time. We found Thomas's knife—it had been dug up or accidentally unearthed somehow, but was basically where he'd left it—and I watched while he flipped it in the air unsheathed and mostly failed to catch it. His mother pulled up around one a.m., with only a few conspiratorial EOB diehards left in the parking lot to keep us company.

"Oh, *Jesus*, Paul," she said when she saw me through the rolled-down passenger window. I imagine she'd planned to deliver some kind of wisecrack, something along the lines of, "Not much fun waiting, is it?" Now, instead, she got out of the car and hurried toward me.

"What happened to you?" she said. I'd never seen her so actively concerned. "Paul, you need stitches."

"It's not that deep," I said.

"How would you know?" she said, which was fair. "I can't give you back to your parents looking like this."

"I think it's an improvement, actually," Thomas muttered to me when we were in the backseat. "Somebody literally knocked that stupid look off your face."

I said nothing. I'd resigned myself to silence in protest of being taken to the hospital for necessary medical attention.

As it happened, I did not *need* stitches. The stitches, the doctor said, were optional at that point, cosmetic. After much debate with my parents, who were, despite my protests, summoned to the Raritan Bay Medical Center in the middle of the night, I chose to keep the scar. It was a stupid decision. I was afraid of the needle, sure. But I also thought that preserving the evidence of the wound might keep me from turning my youth into cheap nostalgia. As if a scar, of all things, were capable of that.

Bad Feelings

scheduled, so I, lacking any pressing obligations, agreed to accompany her and my stepfather Richard to the hospital. She'd gone into the OR at noon and wasn't expected to be out until four, and Richard, God love him, had long exhausted his store of conversation related to traffic and the perfidy of politicians and was now playing solitaire on his laptop. I decided, in an attempt to pass the remaining hours as painlessly as possible, to go to the movies.

I looked up the options on my phone. The choices on offer this February afternoon were not in line with my current interests—a couple of computer-generated kid things, a reboot of an exorcism, the one about the American soldier who, with a heavy heart and exquisite precision, murders a hundred Iraqis. I settled on a movie that had been out for months, the third sequel to a blockbuster adaptation of a young adult book series, of which I had seen none of the previous episodes. It started in ten minutes, but I didn't want to watch the previews anyway.

My mother was probably going to be all right, at least for the day. It was one of many minor surgeries in the course of a major illness. It just so happened to be the one I was home for, and I wasn't acclimated to the anxiety that came with these things. Richard usually called me *after* one of the medical procedures that I hadn't known she was undergoing, which annoyed me even though—and, probably, because—it was for my own emotional good. I was, like my sisters, like my mother, *sensitive*.

Until a few weeks earlier I'd been an editor at a website that mostly published in-depth reviews of food carts around the world; I was laid off when it was purchased by the company of a Koch cousin and folded into a site that focused on branded content directed at wellness enthusiasts. I'd been done with the job anyway, I told myself, and, after finally paying off a decade's worth of credit card debt, I'd been making more money than I absolutely needed. But still: the void was the void. I wanted my mother to be all right in large part so that she would tell me everything was going to be all right.

The theater was on a miserable minor highway in Pennsylvania, packed with chain restaurants and banks and aging non-chain restaurants, the neon signs of which were in various stages of disassembly, intentional or otherwise. The deep sadness of this place, on a sunless afternoon in deep winter, almost started me crying again, as I had been doing more or less continually for months. I held it together. The repetitive contemporary R&B on the radio soothed me.

The theater was distinguished by the presence of a large brick tower in the parking lot, left over from something, I suppose, a prison, or maybe a castle-themed family fun center. There were only a couple of cars in the lot, so I pulled into a spot near the entrance and hurried through the cold to the theater. I was a solid twenty minutes late, which was a little excessive even by the loose standards I held for myself. The skinny kid in the ticket window seemed pleasantly engrossed by his phone, so I decided not to bother him. I told a touch screen what I wanted and it buzzed out a ticket for me. In the lobby there was no one to take the ticket, so I pocketed it for future use. The carpeted hallway was densely coated with smashed popcorn. I followed the trail to my dark, exploding, completely empty theater and took a seat in what I thought to be the dead center.

From what I could gather, a revolution was being fomented, and, naturally, opposed by the oligarchic state. The beautiful young movie star was the chosen one. She had initially been reluctant to join the movement, but she soon saw the need for large-scale armed insurrection and indiscriminate killing. It was better to kill, she learned, than to abandon one's principles, which were not, in this episode at least, explicitly articulated. A famous actor who had recently died appeared in his final role as a conflicted villain—or villainous hero? It was unclear the degree to which his ambivalence was in the script, since it was mostly in his eyebrows.

Attempting to make sense of the on-screen goings-on did not distract me from thinking about my mother. As with classical music, the gulf between my understanding and what I was experiencing was so great that my mind had no choice but to travel elsewhere.

I'd had an emergency appendectomy over the summer, a small opening in my gut through which it seemed an eager passel of physical and mental ailments was allowed to enter. I'd surprised myself with my calm before the surgery: *They have to cut you open*, I thought, *so that's what they'll do.* When it came time for the uncomfortable parts before and after, the prodding and inserting and injecting, I looked away, pretended it was happening to someone else, thought about sex. It wasn't terrifically different from how I got through most things.

I woke up to my mother in my hospital room. She wanted to take me to her hotel, but it turned out I'd developed an infection and needed to spend the night. I wouldn't let her watch her preferred angry news channel so we stared uncomprehendingly at volleyball until I fell asleep again. It was, apparently, the Olympics. I woke up to a screaming white face on the TV, words streaming manically in all directions on the screen. I pleaded for a sitcom, for the sweet release of narcotic death. We looked at gymnasts falling for a while, and by the time I passed out and woke up again some essential part of my confidence in the world's essential stability and goodness had cracked.

Now, watching this movie, I became emotionally invested in the heroine's plight, even as I struggled to understand exactly what she was fighting against. Her boyfriend seemed to be a robot, or maybe just insane. Either way he was a threat to the mission and no match for her other boyfriend, who was blandly beautiful and very committed to the cause. It had been a long time since I'd seen a movie like this, a corporate explosion movie, I mean, and I couldn't tell if it was more violent and disturbing than the ones I'd grown up watching or if I'd just gotten old. What seemed different was the film's insistence on the righteousness of terrorism if it was committed in the name of a good cause. Just a few years before, I thought, this might have been perceived as treasonous, or at least unsuitable for teenagers. Since there was no one else in the audience, it was difficult to know for sure how other people felt, but since the movie had made hundreds of millions of dollars, on top of the hundreds of millions made by the previous installments, not to mention the profits of the books the movies were based on, it seemed fair to assume that lots and lots of people were pretty down with it.

It was passé to feel left behind by the popular modes of expression of the generation that succeeded one's own. It was important to attempt to understand it, to make some kind of truce with the form that had overtaken what you had held dear. I did not want to become my mother, snapping a helpless Wu-Tang CD in half after it was left behind in the family car stereo. But tolerance was not the same as acceptance. I had friends who argued for the profound complexity and depth of the superhero movies. Don't you think it's a little easy? I would say to them. That this thing you love is also the thing that everyone else loves? If all these people love it, isn't it probably stupid? They would respond to me slowly like I was crazy. They told me they admired the structural nuance of serialized storytelling, that the dominant cultural narratives were being subtly undermined by psychosexual dynamics occurring between characters with unorthodox genetic profiles. Well, some of them said that. Usually they just told me that they knew the movies were dumb, but still found them entertaining, and that I should give the dominant culture more of a chance if I didn't want to live a misanthropic empty life. I told them I didn't have time for the dominant culture, which wasn't really true, since mostly I was busy watching sports.

My phone buzzed in my pocket. It was a text from Richard: "no news yet." Well, okay. I felt so sad and lonely that I called Rebecca, the woman I'd been dating for seven years. I knew that she was doing things with her family, but I hoped that she would pick up anyway, from the hiking trail or the rifle range or wherever they all were together. The movie had begun its final descent into air war, and I could barely hear the crackly sonar soundings of my phone as it attempted to make contact with the world outside the theater.

"Hey, babe," I heard faintly. "Everything okay?"

"I'm at a movie," I yelled over the noise.

"Oh," she said. "That's unexpected. How's your mom?"

"In surgery! I just . . . I felt bad."

"I'm sorry. It will be . . . are you *in* the theater? It's very loud."

"There's no one else here," I shouted.

"I think you should finish the movie. We're looking at paintings for my dad. He wants to return the one we got him for Christmas."

"Okay."

"It'll be all right. Try to enjoy the movie."

"It's really bad," I said.

"I know. I'll talk to you later."

"The movie, I mean."

"I know, honey. You'll be okay. I promise."

"Who even are these people, you know? Like, what are they even supposed to represent?"

"I love you. Talk to you later. Give your mom and Richard my love."

"Oh, fuck off," I said once I was sure she'd hung up.

I tried to imagine my family into the action on-screen, Delmore Schwartz–like, but the goings on weren't particularly applicable. My youngest sister was something of a revolutionary. She wore a tuxedo to her high school graduation. She started some kind of Dada art salon and poetry series, which was promptly canceled after one of her classmates read, in protest of the school's social media policy (or something), an uncensored series of racist tweets she'd received. But I didn't see my sister leading the insurrection against the Orwellian dictatorship. Her main personality trait was an unshakeable contrarianism, which was admirable, but it seemed unlikely to draw the masses to her cause. Once the rebels were on her side she'd probably start working with the generals.

The movie ended abruptly, in the midst of rising action, as the heroine raced down a hallway to confront . . . something. I'd known, dimly, that I was buying a ticket to a "Part 1," but I still felt cheated. I suppose people took comfort in knowing that their favorite movie characters would keep coming back again and again, that the adventure never had to stop. It was the hot new stay against death.

I left the theater in a haze of discontent. It wasn't that I cared particularly that I didn't get to find out what happened. I just wanted that feeling of something coming to an end. Even bad old movies—*especially* bad old movies—insisted on the trumpets blaring, true love having been sealed or lost, THE END curling definitively across the screen. No need to walk out on the credits in old movies. They were at the beginning.

When I got outside it was cold, and mostly dark. My car was clustered with a few others now in the front of the lot, like animals keeping warm. I fished around in my pants pockets for my car keys. They weren't there. I ruffled through my trash and receipt and change-filled coat pockets. Nothing. I felt the surge of panic that I always felt in the moment before I ascertained whether or not there was actually a problem. In this case, there was. I did not have my keys. I went back into the theater and went up to the kid at the ticket counter. I explained that I'd left my keys in the theater.

"Let me get a manager," the kid said. His name tag said BENJAMIN.

"I was the only person in there," I said. "I'm just going to run in and check."

"We kind of have this safety protocol?" BENJAMIN said. "I kind of don't want to lose my job?"

So I waited by the entrance, watching the unplayed arcade games shriek and rumble, while he wandered off to find a manager. It would have been very easy at that point to slip down the hall and check out the theater, but I wasn't in the mood to be chastised. The kid was already heading back toward me with a goateed man, his belly straining hard against his maroon, theater-issued button-down shirt.

"Let's go have a look for those keys," the manager said, not breaking stride as he moved toward the theaters. I caught up—he was moving pretty fast for such a large man—and walked alongside him.

"Sorry about this," I said. "Must have just fallen out of my pocket."

"That's my guess," he said. "The cleaning crew's already been through, so we might want to check with them."

"I was the only person in there," I said.

"I understand that, sir," he said. "If you think about it, it probably costs us more to present the film and clean up afterwards than you paid to see it. Pretty good deal for you, huh?"

That didn't seem quite relevant, but I let it go. When we got to the theater, he stopped in front of the propped-open door and swept out his arm with an "after you" flourish. I climbed the auditorium steps briskly. The keys weren't under my seat. I got on my knees and turned on the light on my cell phone. Nothing, not even a stale kernel of popcorn. I went down a row and repeated the search. Nothing.

"They're not there," I said. The manager had been standing against the wall with his arms folded, watching me.

"Are you sure you don't have them on your person?" he said. "Did you have them on your person when you arrived?"

"I drove here," I said.

"Have you checked inside your vehicle?"

"It's locked."

"Is there any possibility that you have locked your keys inside the vehicle?"

"I wouldn't even know how to do that."

"It happens all the time. Leave the keys in the vehicle, vehicle locks automatically, keys are locked inside the vehicle."

"Can we talk to the cleaner?" I said. "I think he'd remember."

The manager ran his hand over his mouth and down over his chin. How fucking busy could his day be? I'd worked in a movie theater as a teenager. When there weren't any customers, there wasn't anything to manage. He pulled a creased piece of paper out of his pocket and examined it.

"He should be in theater five, if he's where he's *supposed* to be," he said. He turned and walked out, leaving me to follow him again.

"I appreciate your help with this," I said as we walked.

"Well, it's imperative, from a managerial standpoint, that this situation gets resolved to your satisfaction."

In theater five, the credits were rolling over a lugubrious martial score. A teenager with a buzz cut was sitting in the seat closest to the door, engrossed in his phone.

"Eli!" the manager shouted. The kid didn't startle, just looked up slowly when he'd finished the text or whatever.

"There was no one in this one," he said. "There was nothing to clean."

The manager walked into the second row, bent over with theatrical effort, and held a straw wrapper in his pinched fingers like a used condom. Eli stood abruptly and grabbed the broom from where it had been leaning against the trash can, sending the dustpan clattering into a row of seats, and swept hurriedly at nothing.

"Okay, Eli, okay," the manager said. "Listen, this gentleman is looking for his car keys. He was in theater eleven, in the show that just got out. Did you collect his car keys?"

"I didn't *collect* anything," Eli said.

"You're sure, when you were sweeping . . ." The manager paused while we all silently acknowledged that Eli had not been sweeping. "You're sure you didn't see any keys?"

"I'd *tell* you, Uncle Jordan. I didn't *see* them."

Jordan turned to me, for the first time signaling apology, or maybe just desperate loneliness, with his eyes.

"I'm running out of ideas here, sir," he said. "Do you have anyone you can call?"

I had Triple A; I had a couple of old friends in town who would probably come help me, if I appeared abject enough. This wasn't something I wanted to explain to my stepfather, under the circumstances, though he was not a judgmental person. He wouldn't be able to help, but he also wouldn't scold me, at least.

"Is this the garbage can you use for all of the theaters?" I said to Eli.

"Um," he said.

My phone buzzed.

"Your Mom is out of surgery," the text read. "Things looking OK. She will be awake in approx 2 hours. Will keep you posted."

I turned to Eli.

"Where are my keys, Eli?" I tried to sound forceful, but it was probably closer to hysteria.

"Dude, what?" he said.

"Sir, I understand your frustration," Jordan said. "Let's go down to the office and file a lost-and-found report. That way if your keys turn up, we'll have everything ready to go here for you."

I didn't want to break down weeping in front of this man and his nephew, so I plunged my arm down inside the tall garbage can in front of me. It was mostly popcorn, though it was plenty wet in there, too, especially down toward the bottom. I gripped and ungripped my fist, mashing the stuff in the bin deeper into goo. Of course there wasn't anything that felt like keys, even as my hand kept voyaging, grasping for anything solid. Jordan and Eli watched me pitilessly, unsurprised. Did this happen often? I pulled my reeking arm out of the can and tried to speak coherently.

"But where could they have *gone*?" I said. "I mean, outside of your capacity as *the manager* and all that, what do you think *happened*? Just as a person? They didn't just *disappear*, right?" My voice was shaking so badly that I had to stop.

"My guess?" the manager said, after he'd paused to make sure I was done. "You're going to find them where you least expect it."

"Do you have *back* pockets?" Eli said, his youthful sympathy blooming like a flower on a corpse.

I patted my back pocket in desperate hope. *Thanks, kid!* But no. Nothing there.

"My mother's in the hospital," I said.

Jordan nodded. "I figured it was something," he said.

I followed his now slow-moving buttocks to his office and began to write down my information on a photocopied form with "Lost it at the movies?" printed across the top.

"Hey, man," Jordan said softly. I looked up from my writing. (What *was* my address?)

"Check this out."

He unbuttoned the first three buttons of his shirt and pulled the fabric aside to reveal his chest. FUCK CANCER was tattooed in green Gothic script beneath his collarbone. The skin around it was pale and hairless. Did he shave it? He certainly kept it out of the sun.

"That's great," I said.

"*Fuck. Cancer.* Right?" he said. He looked me deep in the eyes, desperate again. "Just. Fuck it."

My mother didn't have cancer. I nodded solemnly.

"Thank you," I said. "You're right."

He slowly rebuttoned his shirt and turned to his computer in the corner, signaling, apparently, the end of our business. I filled out the rest of the surprisingly detailed form—office fax number?—and put it on the desk.

"So you'll let me know if you find anything?" I said. "Or get any, um, tips?"

"Any information we receive will be conveyed to you in a timely fashion," he said without turning to me.

I walked quietly out of the office and back outside.

At my car, I pressed my nose against the cold driver-side window. *Could* the keys be in there? It was too dark to tell. I went in my wallet to find my Triple-A card. They'd tow it somewhere, I supposed. To my mother's house. I'd get a new key. Life would trundle unhappily forward, making many bureaucratic stops along the way. Maybe Jordan would call me tomorrow—that little rascal Eli *had* found the keys, and he'd been caught ghost-riding my whip in the dawn's early light. Maybe that faint possibility was reason enough to leave the car behind.

Across the parking lot, I could see the corporate pizza outpost, lit up and empty, where I'd spent a lot of time over the course of a particularly tedious summer. The food it served was nearly inedible, but the bar was suspiciously well stocked with local beer. One suspected that someone was getting away with something. It felt like a long time since I'd gotten away with anything.

I crossed the frozen concrete, made it through two sets of doors. A late-period Red Hot Chili Peppers song was playing over the sound system, always a sign of excellent things to come. The restaurant was nearly empty, but there were a few bodies scattered through the bar area.

I ducked into a table at the window, out of which I could mostly see my own reflection. At the bar was an elderly white man wearing a Knicks Starter jacket, maybe over a hospital gown, and a very thin woman sitting as far from him as possible, both of them drinking from short glasses and craning their necks toward a sports recap program playing silently across three TVs above the bar. When I was young, I had prayed, without having the words for it, not to be one of these people. And I wasn't, I told myself, not really. A waiter noticed me and swooped over, making big strides on his long legs.

"You all set here?" he said, glancing down at the laminated menu that had apparently been in front of me the entire time. He was tall and balding and radiating what felt like actual generosity, unless my disposition was simply softening with the promise of alcohol.

"I think so," I said. I smiled at him searchingly. I hadn't looked at the menu. He smiled back more warily, probably wondering whether I was going to tackle him or start bellowing obscenities.

"So what can I get you?" he said.

"Oh," I said. It seemed important to get it right on the first try. "I just . . ."

"I'll give you a minute," he said.

"No, no," I said. I was crying a little bit, enough that I couldn't really read the menu, but I hoped he wouldn't notice. "I'll just have the, um, let's see here . . . Hop Head? Hop Head presents Hops and Dreams?"

"Well . . ." He paused. The generosity in him was flickering. But it *had* been there, I was sure of it.

"That's not on the menu," he said, like he was disappointed that he couldn't accommodate me. I'd just been saying words that sounded like an expensive beer. I nodded grimly.

"It sounds like you want something hoppy," he continued. "I'll bring you something I think you'll like. Sound good?"

"That . . . that would be perfect," I said.

And I thought: *Was that so hard?* I'd made some sounds, and what I'd wanted would now be manifested, even if I hadn't done everything in the traditional manner. With an appropriate amount of goodwill, I could, in fact, be quite easily accommodated.

I looked at the TV. Buy gold! The waiter brought the beer. He was beaming, triumphant. It was all going so well.

"Thanks very much," I said, crisp and businesslike. The waiter gave a little bow and went back to the bar.

Now that I'd accomplished this, I thought, I might be better equipped to handle whatever came next. I took my first sip. It tasted strongly of dirt and metal, with an overlay of grain alcohol. Something was terribly wrong with the tap, or with my sense of taste, or with any world that could produce such a beverage. I took another sip, hoping it might start to make some kind of sense. It tasted even worse.

A Dog Named Jesus

LESLIE BOUGHT A BOTTLE OF gin at a dimly lit casino liquor store and drove it to Allison's house. She'd just bombed another job interview, her third in two weeks, this time for an assistantship at the Montana Wolf Conservancy. She rapped along with Biggie, who was, as usual, asking the tough questions: What *was* she going to do when Big Poppa came for her? It was badass job-getting music, but it worked just as well now that she hadn't gotten a job. All the worst people worked for nonprofits, anyway.

She let herself in through her friend's unlocked front door and found Allison's shaggy boyfriend Clyde and a bearded man she didn't know sitting in the living room, drinking beer and sorting piles of dried mushrooms into piles on the coffee table.

"Oh hey," Clyde said. "Boy, am I glad you're not a cop! Jake, this is Leslie. She's the best."

"I'm the best," Leslie said.

She held out her hand and Jake grasped it weakly for a

moment, giving her an appraising, sidelong smirk before returning his attention to the mushrooms.

"Jake works with me out at the Book Barn," Clyde said.

"Well, they keep me in the back," Jake said. "I sort through the new arrivals, organize the decent books, throw away the bad ones."

"You don't *throw them away*," Clyde said.

"I *arrange for the donation* of the shitty books, thank you."

"I think I'd be good in the back room, if I wasn't un-hireable," Leslie said.

"Yeah, I'd be a lot of things if I was someone else, too," Jake said.

"Being such a dummy must really limit your options," Leslie said. "Where's Allison?"

"Cookin' stuff," Clyde said.

Leslie found her in the kitchen stirring something in a large pot. The kitchen was well tended but not obnoxiously so. There were copper pans hanging over the stove and a conspicuous spice rack, but the space projected use and love, not just curatorial intention. Leslie didn't cook much herself. If she'd spent the day drinking gin and reading about Mark Rothko, or, you know, *Syria*, how could she justify wasting another hour measuring out ingredients or whatever you were supposed to do? It took all of her energy to remember to *eat* the food in the house before it went bad, forget *cooking* it.

"It's our underemployed baby!" Allison said. "And her big bottle of gin!"

Leslie went straight to the refrigerator.

"Christ, do you not have any tonic?" she said. She took out a bottle of grapefruit juice and poured liquor into two glasses.

"You're not presenting as triumphant," Allison said.

"The interview guy asked me if I wanted to change the world," Leslie said. She tipped a splash of juice into both glasses. "I said, Um . . . for the better? There was this long pause, and finally he goes . . . Is there any other way?"

She gave Allison her gin and juice and took a big sip of her own. Allison grimaced.

"I wanted mine weeknight-strength," she said.

The Grateful Dead played from the boom box on the counter. The Dead were one of many things Leslie tolerated only because she loved Allison. Others included tea, yoga, and feeling generally all right about life.

Jake and Clyde wandered into the kitchen and sat down at the table.

"Is the food ready yet?" Clyde said. "I don't know about you guys, but what I'm ready for? Is *food*."

"You from around here, Jake?" Leslie said.

"Naw, I moved from Seattle with my girlfriend when she got into the forestry Ph.D.," Jake said. "But we broke up last year."

"Man, I'm sure you can do better than some, like, wood nymph, anyway," Leslie said. "I wouldn't sweat it."

"Your East Coast ignorance is somehow getting *worse*," Clyde said.

"I don't care how long I stay here," Leslie said. "I'm not going to be *impressed* by forests. Trees are cool. Necessary, even. But that's as far as I'll go."

Jake didn't smile. "It was a bad breakup, but I still have a lot of respect for what she's trying to do," he said.

"Oh man," Clyde said, deliberately shifting the conversation. "Today a guy came into the store asking for a book to give to his girlfriend. He says, 'What's the one about the famous magician? The one with Leonardo DiCaprio?' And I'm thinking, I'm thinking."

"Oh no," Allison said.

"And suddenly I realize what he's talking about. I ask him, 'Do you mean . . . *The Great Gatsby*?' And he's all relieved. 'Yes! Dude, thank you!'"

"It *is* a pretty misleading title," Jake said.

"It should be about a magician," Leslie said. "A magician who hypnotizes women into thinking he's Leonardo DiCaprio."

"We didn't have *Gatsby*, so I gave him *Tropic of Cancer*," Clyde said. "I told him it was an island hospital romance."

"*He went to the islands for love*," Allison said. "*But what he found . . . was cancer.*"

"Well, it's not like this girlfriend actually reads books, anyway," Leslie said. "Girlfriend, in quotes. Sorry we're being such assholes."

Jake was sitting back with a polite smile on his face.

"At least he was trying, right?" he said.

Leslie wasn't a big fan of the new sincerity that had bludgeoned her supposed generation, but she could be down with decency, if she had to be.

"Everyone respects everyone," Allison said in her kindergarten-teacher voice. She handed out bowls and they lined up at the stove.

———

It was nearly dark and they lay on the floor, full of lentils, listening to *After the Gold Rush*.

"Neil fucking *Young*, man," Allison said. "He knows only *love* can break your heart."

"I think sadness could, too, though," Leslie said. "Where's that Jake?"

"He's smoking a cigarette," Clyde said. "Cuz he wants to *die*."

"Hey, me, too," Leslie said.

She went out the back door through the kitchen and put her hand on Jake's shoulder.

"Gimme," she said.

He handed her one and lit it with a Mariners lighter.

"I'm getting tired of this town, you know?" she said. She let out a burst of smoke. "I mean, it's fucked up, because obviously it's better than most places. But sometimes it's like, God, what am I *doing*? I'm just going to be *forgotten* here. Sorry, you seem cool so I'm ranting at you."

"Who's going to forget you?" Jake said.

"People in cities. The old, fake America. I should move back to New York and be a brand consultant or whatever."

"Yeah, follow your dreams," Jake said.

"Well, what are you doing?"

"I don't know, man. Working on some poetry. Figuring out how to dedicate my energy toward something moderately positive. Picking up some paychecks when I can."

"Could be worse," she said.

"Probably ends badly, though," he said. "Gonna be a

lotta slow singing, and flower bringing, et cetera." The man knew his Biggie—a sign? He put out his cigarette and dropped it in the Mason jar full of butts by the back door.

"But hey, look," he said. He put his hand on her shoulder. "Fuck it. I'm going to this very low-key wedding tomorrow in Wyoming and need to leave at, like, the crack of dawn. Long shot, but: Do you want to *come*, by any chance?"

"Sorry, what is it?" Leslie said.

"My friends are getting married at this hot springs. It's kind of a camping thing? The kind of thing that can be crashed without fear of reprisal, I mean? It's going be real fun, but it *is* like seven hours away. And I realize you probably have shit to do, and that this might be way too weird. You just seem cool is all."

Leslie didn't totally appreciate being put on the spot, but the fact was, no, it wasn't too weird—she was in Missoula. And this maybe fell into the category of decisions that were romantic and worth doing but not completely awful and full of shit, if that category existed.

"That sounds kind of great, actually," she said. "You'd need to pick me up . . . when?"

"A little before five a.m.?" he said. "That's pretty soon."

"Not soon enough," Leslie said. She raised her chin to see if he'd kiss her, but he didn't.

She woke to her alarm at 4:30. She dumped out the books and dirty clothes that had been in her duffel bag since her last trip home six months earlier and hurriedly filled it with different dirty clothes, a musty bathing suit, and books she hoped she might someday want to read. *The Man Without Qualities*? Check. Probably wouldn't need volume two, though. She put on a mostly unrumpled flowery sundress that it was too cold out to wear now, and would be again by nightfall, but she threw her parka over it and called it a day. She saw headlights at the curb. All of her dishes were in the sink and her clothes and books were now strewn across the apartment. She locked the door behind her for the first time in weeks.

Jake was wearing a baseball cap and a bulky checked flannel coat. With his truck and his beard, out there in the dark, Leslie would not normally have been happy to see him. Another mountain creep waiting through the night for someone to come out, or, worse, working up the dubious courage to go in. She hopped up into the smoke-smelling cab. A chubby little blue heeler occupied the space between them.

"This is Alamo," Jake said. "Never forget."

The second disc of *Exile on Main St.* was playing low on the stereo as they drove out of town, the spooky voodoo song about Jesus. She was glad Jake liked *Exile*. Not that anybody didn't.

Leslie tried to keep her eyes open and respond to Jake's chat—mostly stuff about this Kelly girl who'd chosen a pair of polyamorous forestry colleagues over him and Alamo— but was lulled toward sleep by the warmth and motion of the truck. She napped after she was assured, via a McDonald's coffee stop, that Jake wasn't going to drift off and run the truck over the edge of a mountain. She woke up with the sour taste of sleep in her mouth and the sun shining in her eyes.

"Are we close?" she said.

"Closer than we were," said Jake.

They were passing through a dune-patched stretch of dirt, pretty, if you were into desolation. They found a country station and Leslie resisted the urge to extemporize on the political implications of twenty-first-century female revenge narratives, namely that they were a backdoor endorsement of the anti-feminist swill that was washing ashore in America of late. Chicks are some crazy, dude. They'll smash your shit if you break up with them. Better to keep letting them cook and clean for you if that's what makes them happy. Jake sang along to the boy songs about backyards and barbecues in a chinny voice that indicated he recognized they were awful. Still, he knew all the words.

At a gas station on tribal land, a trio of smoking cowboy-hatted men eyed her. *On my way to squat briefly over a cold, filthy toilet, gents. Welcome to join, if that's your thing.* She got internally confrontational out here whenever she got outside of Missoula, and sometimes when she was still in town, too. It was rarely overt, but there was still a lot of implied Western bullshit going on, as much from the older women as from the men. Something like, Shut up and get tough. She got it. She'd never gutted an elk. Never fucking would.

Jake was at the counter when she walked out of the bathroom.

"Are you buying a gas station breakfast sandwich?" she said.

"Um, no?" he said. "It just . . . looks that way? Do *you* want one?"

"That's okay. I'll just get these." She threw a bag of honey-roasted peanuts on the counter. "And I'm going to get a coffee, too."

"Am I paying for this?" he said.

"You don't have to," she said. "Sorry. I can put it on my card."

"I was just kidding," he said.

"Okay. I mean, I kind of figured it's, like, two bucks, and I'll get the next one or whatever."

"It is seriously not in any way a problem," he said.

Jake paid for the snacks and they got back in the truck. Terry Gross was interviewing Ray Davies for the hundredth anniversary of "Waterloo Sunset" or something. Re: the death of chivalry in financial matters, Leslie was ambivalent. In the twilight of the days with her last ex, he'd been unemployed, so she had uncomplainingly paid for most of their living expenses. When he'd had money, from freelance work or a birthday check, he'd done his best to pick up the slack. If you added it up, she'd spent way more than he had over the course of the relationship, but it wasn't a major point of contention. When she thought seriously about it, she realized she wouldn't have been happy with someone who thought it was his "duty" to pay for her, but more because it was a proxy for other chauvinist qualities than because she actually cared about the money. She *really* didn't care, or at least was so invested in the idea that she didn't that she was willing to spend more than she should on a doomed live-in relationship. And she wasn't resentful about it now? You know, that's a *great* question, Terry.

They arrived at the address an hour before the wedding was supposed to start. It was not, as Leslie had imagined, a steaming pool in the middle of the woods, but rather looked to be a saloon-and-hotel kind of deal off the very dead Main Street of a one-street town. Jake parked his truck between two mud-caked Outbacks and clipped a bow tie onto Alamo's collar before letting him out to pee against a tire.

"Where's the hot spring?" Leslie said.

"It's one of those pool ones. They pipe it in," Jake said. "Don't worry, it'll probably still smell like sulfur."

The wedding guests lingering in front of the main building displayed a wide sartorial range. There were two men in full tuxes, though their top hats indicated some degree of irony, and a couple of women, who looked to be their dates, in evening gowns. But they were chatting with a group that looked practically indigent, with worn-out pants and tattered shirts and mangy dogs roaming at their feet. The median look was something like Leslie and Jake's—clean, decent clothes, with a vaguely Western flavor. Black jeans and fancy belt buckles, pearl snap buttons, boots. The men were bearded, the women wild-haired. It was, Leslie thought, an unusually attractive group.

Jake approached a very tall man with a thick beard and long, dirty-blond hair pulled into a bun. He was dressed in blue denim from head to toe. Jake gave him a tight one-armed hug.

"Leslie, this is Marlon," he said. "He makes very cool music. And cocktails and sculptures, and probably some other stuff, too."

"Hey," Marlon said. "I guess I'm a real Renaissance fair. Are you, like, Jake's girlfriend?"

"I'm, like, his semi-idealized, potentially dangerous impulse invite," Leslie said.

"You want to get stoned before this thing starts?" Marlon said.

"Definitely."

She walked with Jake and Marlon, and Marlon's silent barefoot companion Yvette, through the bar and the spacious, dark-wood-paneled dance hall, out past the small row of motel rooms, to the field adjacent to the rows of white folding chairs. There were a few tents out in the field, with more being raised presently by the more hirsute guests. Jake gave a sharp whistle and Alamo, chased grinningly by a matted golden retriever, raced toward them from around the corner of the building.

"That's where me and Yvie are sleeping," Marlon said, gesturing toward an expertly pinioned blue teepee set off a hundred yards from the others.

"Really worried about privacy, huh?" Leslie said.

"It's more the opposite, I think," Yvette said. These were the first words Leslie had heard her speak. She had bright red hair, short on the sides, with a tiny ducktail pompadour in the middle. Her face was tan and weathered, drawing out the brightness of her deep green eyes.

"What do you mean?" Leslie said.

"A lighthouse," said Yvette. "We want every ship in

shape. You know, shipshape ships and shops? For the *con-scientious* consumer of nautical know-how?"

"Yvette's trying to make her life into a poem," Marlon said. "A really fucked-up poem."

Jake lowered his voice to a rumbling monotone. "I figured you'd be okay with a kind of unconventional scene, yeah?"

They stood in a circle behind Marlon's tent and passed a bowl.

"How do you know the wedding people?" Leslie said.

"I was in a band with Keith for a while," Marlon said. "In Spokane. We're going to play a surprise set later. It's gonna be like, Hey, Keith, remember these songs you wrote like ten years ago? No? Well, we've been practicing for weeks, so you better *catch up, bro.*"

"I wonder if he'll appreciate that," Leslie said. "On his wedding day and all."

"On a bright blue day in early June, I met a dog named Jesus," Yvette recited, as if she'd been cued. "And though I knew it not that hour, I entered into wonder true."

"Those are the first lines of Yvette's book," Marlon said. "She's been honing them. Relentlessly."

"What happens next?" Leslie said.

"Salvation," Yvette said. "And dog stuff. It's based on market research plus my own unique blend of humor and wisdom."

"Sounds great."

"I have a lot of confidence in my approach."

The weed, as could be expected from Yvette's comportment, was quite potent. Despite having achieved Missoulastrength tolerance, Leslie was now close to being way too stoned after a few hits. People were speaking at unpredictable intervals and she tried to time her laughs and smiles to when they finished their sentences. She didn't think she was getting it right. Marlon was suddenly talking about how his brother, or cousin, died in a car accident, and she tried to make herself look serious by frowning deeply, like Obama used to, but that thought made her smile, and then she was thinking of herself as a cartoon frog trying to smile, with the frog's lips turning upside down every time they went all the way up, and then flipping over again into a frown. And then once the frog was in full frown, it saw a fly and zipped its tongue out and caught it, which made it smile again, until the smile turned over. She jolted herself out of this and saw that Marlon and Yvette were walking away. She was standing in the field holding Jake's sweaty hand. She let go abruptly.

"Where's my camera?" she said. But then she remembered she hadn't brought a camera. "Nothing," she said a couple of seconds later.

"What?" Jake said.

"I. Don't. Have. One."

"Okay. I don't know what you're talking about."

They walked back to the parking lot and got their bags and camping stuff out of Jake's truck. She helped—well, held the stakes, mostly, while Alamo tried to pull them out of the ground with his teeth—as Jake set up their tent in the shadow of Marlon and Yvette's. Leslie laid out their sleeping bags side by side.

"We could just wait this thing out from in here," she

said. She patted the ground heavily, which she'd meant to seem enticing, but now struck her as aggressive and insane.

"We have to go watch the love," Jake said.

Leslie felt Jake's proximity—his aura, if she believed in auras—as a benign, protective thing, and this made her think of Allison in Missoula, and also to wish precipitously, despite the sunshine, that she was having a drink in her backyard now instead of whatever this was. She loved Allison, and Clyde, or at least what they became when they were together and talking to her. It was real.

She crawled out of the tent—*swish swish rustle.*

"I'm ready for the cleaving," Leslie said.

"Hey, great word," said Jake.

The sky grew cloudy as they put Alamo in the truck— "His animal kingdom," Jake assured her. They arrived at their seats just as a fiddler and a mandolin player started in on a very loose interpretation of the "Wedding March." A moment later, everyone stood as the bride, wearing a short brown peasant dress and a massive white sun hat, floated toward the makeshift altar.

Two hours later, Marlon was at her side again. For the toasts and dinner, Jake had been on her left and Corinne, a woman who talked mostly about her travels to Hawaii for obscure fund-raising purposes, had been on her right. But ever since dessert, Jake had been making the rounds, catching up with friends, or—who knew?—just randomly bothering people he liked the look of, and, for two discrete periods of time now, Marlon had been next to her, making laconic comments about the people in their line of sight. The weed had worn off a while back, but she was well on her way to being drunk, and she wondered whether or not she actually enjoyed Marlon's company. He was making her laugh, but was he funny? She was attracted to him, but was he good-looking? The answers felt just out of reach.

Jake, on the other hand: She'd decided she was interested in him, even though it was possible that he wasn't that interesting. Or, well, okay. The central question about *him* was whether or not his relative lack of first-rate entertainment value (as measured by quips, theories, etc.) was made up for by reservoirs of feelings and insights that were too subtle to be revealed in this slam-bang atmosphere. In any case, he lacked the awareness to do anything about Marlon hitting on her, though maybe he was just evolved, or trusted that Yvette's presence would discourage action. But what was Yvette to Marlon, anyway? Leslie caught a glimpse of her at a table in the corner, nodding off and then jerking into consciousness like a kid in algebra class.

"I don't think it's cruel, necessarily, to say that *that* woman looks like a *particular* dog," Marlon was saying. "Not in the—what is it?—*pejorative* sense, but just, like, she looks like a poodle, right? Shouldn't we have reached a place, as a society, certain egregious examples notwithstanding, where *anyone* can look like a dog?"

"Insisting you're not an asshole doesn't actually protect you from being one," Leslie said.

"Shit," he said. "I keep noticing that being a person involves, like, frequent adjustments to your actual circumstances."

"That's an extremely basic realization. That's something you learn when you're a small child."

Marlon smirked. He was saying dumb things just so she would chastise him, and she was playing into it.

"I should go set up for our performance," he said. "I guess we shouldn't sound-check if it's supposed to be a surprise. Whatever. It doesn't matter. How drunk do I seem to you?"

"A regular amount, I guess?"

"Oh, do you want to be a, like, go-go girl? You know, dance around us on the stage and stuff, like the sixties?"

"Absolutely not."

"Just thought I should ask," he said.

He loped off toward the front of the room. Such long legs! She glanced over at a nearby table and saw Jake making expansive hand gestures—head! exploding!—in between a poshly dressed man and woman. There was a free seat at the table, so she ambled over and took it.

Jake was finishing his story. "So, yeah, no more political fund-raisers for me."

The man next to him slapped the table hard, rattling the glasses. To convey violent amusement, presumably?

The woman on his left said, "But seriously, Jake, if you're ever willing to give it another shot, we'd certainly accept your *money*."

This woman was blond and very pretty, but she was so done up that it wasn't clear what she actually looked like. Even if the fancy clothes were some kind of joke, her dress was clearly expensive, and it fit her perfectly, like a sexy Halloween costume. And she was actually some kind of political shill? It transpired that they were Dora and Rich-

A DOG NAMED JESUS

ard, a married consulting partnership. Leslie drank deep from someone's abandoned glass of white wine.

"When are we going to get married, Jake?" she said. The consultants pantomimed curiosity.

"I thought we said next summer," he said. "Though fall weddings are very in on the East Coast. And I know how much you love the Jersey Shore in November."

"It's true," Leslie said. "When the gray sky hits the brown water just right, it's almost like you're in Rhode Island."

"When did you really start dating?" Richard said. "Jake said you met yesterday, but I don't believe him."

"These are the last true things I'll ever say," Leslie said. "We met last night. I've never kissed him. I'm not sure I'm going to. I don't remember his last name, if I ever knew it."

"McLaughlin," Jake said. He leaned over Richard and kissed Leslie briefly on the mouth.

"Well, there you have it," Leslie said.

"Right," said Dora skeptically.

A burst of feedback cut through the room and everyone at the table turned to the stage. Marlon was standing at the microphone with a guitar; two other long-haired wedding guests were on drums and bass.

"Keith," Marlon said. "Congratulations on getting married. The, uh, wedding band is running a little bit late. So come on up here, buddy. You are *fucked*."

Some time later: the promised hot spring. In the dark, with spotlights throwing shadows against high cement walls,

the pool felt to Leslie like a POW camp in a barely remembered black-and-white movie. She'd continued drinking
through all of the dancing (to a soul band that was margin-
ally better than Marlon's), and the alcohol had flooded her
brain with foreboding. She blamed the darkness.

Jake was being weird to her now, or maybe he'd just gotten too drunk, too. Instead of bantering, he just nodded in
response to things she said and looked over at Yvette, as if
for confirmation. He seemed into her, and maybe he hoped
Leslie would take Marlon out of the picture. Or maybe he
and Marlon had agreed to trade women while she was out
of earshot. An exchange of cargo, like in the *Iliad*. Marlon
and Yvette were currently giggling at each other, her sitting
on the edge of the pool in her tiny white bikini, all lines and
angles, him floating in the pale light, facing her. Leslie was
submerged up to her shoulders and starting to feel too hot.
When she looked at Yvette, took in her unbearable light-
ness, she felt like an inflatable pool toy. There was a crew
of boisterous family members in the shallow end blasting
Journey songs from a boom box. Jake kept going underwater, sinking to the bottom of the pool, and then bursting
rapidly up to the surface. It was startling and unattractive.
Alamo raced along the edge of the pool, barking every time
anyone bobbed too close to Jake.

"I think I'm happy," Yvette said, as if someone had
asked. "I countenance my surroundings, and I formulate an
emotional state. It's a two-step solution."

"It's not required," Marlon said.

"Yeah, I know," Yvette said. "That's a good thing to remember. You get to feeling like you have to account for

everything. *You've* been married, Mar. You don't have any-thing to talk about so you spend all your time, like, explain-ing exactly *how* you arrived in your emotional state. Because if it's for some unacceptable reason, that's apparently some-thing your husband needs to know about."

"You're married?" Leslie said. She floated closer.

"I'm separated. *Very* separated. I'd say, if you're think-ing about getting married? Just, like, have a drink and read a book by yourself for a couple hours. See how good it feels."

This was, by a long shot, the most focused Yvette had been all night.

"I wish *my* ex had wanted to read," Marlon said. "I'd have been, like, full speed ahead, baby."

"Well, yeah, but that's the thing. Your husband always wants you to do the opposite of what you *do* want to do. If I'd wanted to go to the farmers' market, or whatever the fuck your Katie was always doing, Zachary would've wanted me to stay home and read a book."

Leslie's perception of Marlon and Yvette had tilted and she didn't feel capable of grappling with it and speaking co-herently at the same time. There were so many ways to deal with stupid, crippling loneliness, so few of them good. You struggled until you failed, and then you started over again at the beginning. The best option was probably to com-plicate your attachments to such a degree that they hardly seemed like attachments at all.

She floated over to Jake, who was staring fixedly at Yvette.

"You okay, man?" she said.

"*Oh* yeah," he said automatically.

"Hey, look at me," Leslie said. "Why did you invite me to this thing?"

He looked unfocusedly in her direction.

"Thought you were cool," he said. "Wanted company."

"But not anymore?"

He dunked his head underwater, then reemerged and flicked his wet hair in her direction.

"Of course," he said.

He said it as if it had no connection to what she'd asked. She decided she would try one more time to be straight with him.

"I feel kind of alone, you know?" she said.

Jake's eyes drifted back to Yvette. "I get that," he said.

There was a loud thunder crack and a burst of lightning that looked to be very nearby. Leslie hoisted herself up out of the pool, with Marlon and Jake close behind. A couple of tall figures in the shallow end had their arms raised to the sky, defiant. One of them extended his middle fingers. "We don't give a damn, we don't give a fuck!" he yelled, until a woman—girlfriend? aunt?—waded back and dragged him out by the wrist. Leslie wrapped herself in a towel and tried to stop shivering. Jake watched the shuddering sky with sincere-looking solemnity. Maybe he was composing a poem. Was it wrong to assume he was a bad poet? Probability was on her side. But would it kill her to be a little more generous? It *might* kill her to keep standing in a dripping puddle during a lightning storm.

"Sanctuary!" Yvette yelled, and she and the two boys joined the pack of dogs and guests sprinting toward the field. Leslie watched them go, and then went back to looking at the sky. She stayed still. *If it be now, it's not to come,* she thought, or something like that. She watched the lightning striking the world, sometimes far away, sometimes, it seemed, close enough to touch. No one came looking for her. After half an hour, or three hours, or three weeks, she realized that the storm had passed and that she was shivering uncontrollably. She walked briskly into the lodge, through the now-dark and empty hall where the reception had been, to the bar, which was occupied by Richard, the political consultant, still in his suit, sitting with his back to the wall at a mixed table of ruffians and respectable-looking people.

"Hey, the mystery date," Richard said. The others at the table turned toward her and she became very aware that she was in a dripping bathing suit (a modest maroon one-piece, but still), wrapped in a towel, in a room of fully dressed men.

"I am one hundred percent dehydrated," Leslie said.

"Sounds like you should stick to beer," Richard said. "We've got an extra one. I don't know who ordered it."

"I did," said a gray-bearded man with a black ponytail. "It turned out it was fucking cider. You can have it, piss in it, whatever."

Leslie took the seat nearest to the full glass. The cider was still cold, and it tasted wonderful, dry and slightly carbonated, barely sweet. She was grateful to whoever didn't want it.

"Where's Thing Two?" Leslie said to Richard. "Girl you?"

"Dora went to bed," he said. "We managed to snag the one free room in the lodge. All it took was money."

"It's storming out there, but I'm medium confident that our tent is pretty much watertight," she said. "Jake's campy, right? *Un campesino?*"

"He looks it," Richard said. "I mean, he's got a beard. You really don't know him, huh?"

"Is there anything to know?"

"Trust but verify, I guess."

"And you?" she said.

"I try."

It was interesting to flirt with unavailable men with whom one had little in common. It was an active opportunity to imagine the world fresh. It would be a *more* active opportunity, though, if moving her head too quickly didn't make her dizzy.

"Are these all your buddies?" she said, raising her chin at the table.

"These guys are literally in town from Portland to film a Nike commercial," Richard said. "You can thank them for your night on the blasted hearth. Heath?"

"Whichever," Leslie said. "Cheers, sweatshop bozos."

She drained her glass.

"So any chance *you're*, um, putting out tonight?" she said.

He cocked his head. "Are you asking me for money?" he said lightly.

"No," she said. "The other thing."

"I think Dor finished the blow, unfortunately," he said. *Blow?* Did people say *blow?*

"I wanted to sleep in your guys's bed," she said. "As,

like, a kinky Good Samaritan thing. That's what everyone's into now, no? I was mostly messing with you."

He kept his eyes on her, smiled a tight politician's smile.

"You're welcome, definitely, to sleep in our room, since
it's so awful out. I'll hit the floor, or we can see if we can get
a cot or something. That's absolutely doable."

Leslie felt the tedium of the night bearing down on her.

"It's all right, man," she said. "I'll do the hearth."

She stood up abruptly, her vision going dark for a moment, and walked almost-steadily out the side door, around
the building, and out toward the tents in the light rain. Marlon's teepee was lit up, and she could see shadows inside, so
she opened the flap. Jake and Yvette sat hunched toward
each other, their foreheads nearly touching across Marlon's
sleeping body. Alamo, sprawled on his side, clocked her entrance with the minutest lift of his head, then returned to
his rest.

"Um," said Jake. "We're actually having a kind of private conversation."

Yvette looked up at her with red, shrunken eyes. "It's
fine," she said. "I'm just having a deeply conventional, terrible time and I don't want to talk about it with too many
people."

"I put my Mariners hat on top of my tent so you could
find it," Jake said.

Some fortification in her, which she hadn't quite known
existed, was breached.

"You want me to go sleep by myself while you fuck
Yvette back to mental clarity?"

"It's healthy to be jealous," Yvette said. "But ultimately fruitless. In the sense of an orchard bearing fruit, I mean."

Marlon was sleeping silently, no sign of life. Was he dreaming? Or in that darkness that enough drugs and booze and exhaustion can bring if you combine them right? He seemed content, whichever it was.

"Listen, I don't care what you guys do," Leslie said. "But I'm staying here. I want to be lying down, and near people, okay? I'm going to lie down here next to Marlon and I'm going to go to sleep. You can keep talking here or lie down too, or sleep or have sex or talk more in the other tent, or go for a walk and come back and then lie down in here. That's what I'm going to do, okay?"

She slipped her shoes off and took the towel from her shoulders. Her bathing suit was still wet, so she hurriedly pulled the straps down, peeled the suit to her waist, and stepped out through the bottom. She felt a momentary spike of excitement as she stood up, naked, in front of Jake and Yvette. Stripped bare, finally. Then she crawled under Marlon's unzipped sleeping bag and pressed herself against his clothed body.

"Are you okay with this?" Jake said.

"She seems like a really nice person," Yvette said.

They went back to their conversation—Yvette was having money problems, and her mentally ill parents were making things worse. Leslie listened to the murmuring over her head until, finally warmed through, she dreamed the wedding over again, better.

She woke up in the dark with someone spooning her

from behind. Definitely, well, a man. Marlon. To her right, other bodies were hard at work. She pressed herself against Marlon and he threw an arm over her.

"Hey, Marlon," she whispered.

"Huh," he said.

"Do you want to have sex?"

Silence.

"I'm kind of asleep," he said finally.

She turned so that she was facing him.

"Jake and Yvette are having sex," she said.

"It's a mitzvah," he said.

"No, it's not," she said. He seemed to be sleeping again, or pretending to. She felt a gut-punch of homesickness, the worst she'd felt since summer camp.

"Marlon," she said. "Let me suck your cock."

There was a long pause during which she regretted saying it, but would not allow herself to take it back.

"Now?" he said.

"Yeah," she said. "Don't you want that?"

Silence.

"I really need to sleep," Marlon said.

"Come on," she said. She made her voice an octave higher, slowed it to a sluggish drawl. "Wouldn't that be nice for you? I bet it would."

She put her hand on his leg.

"You don't have to do that," he mumbled.

She turned this over in her head. It was incredible, she concluded, the number of ways one could be condescended to.

"I don't have to do anything, actually," she said.

She turned away from him and edged herself closer to Jake and Yvette.

"There?" Jake said.

"Yeah," said Yvette. "More."

"Like that?"

"Yeah."

She listened as things progressed, not terribly discreet to begin with, and becoming less so. She contemplated reaching out and touching them, grabbing Yvette's foot, digging her nail down Jake's spine. Once, in college, she'd come home from a bar and playfully launched herself into her roommate Patricia's bed, only to discover that she'd interrupted a delicate, first-time session with the boy who would, much later, become Patricia's husband. She'd pretended ignorance for an extra couple of seconds, enough time to absorb their warmth and embarrassment, and then fled the room. She'd taken refuge in the bed of a boy down the hall, but she'd made it absolutely clear: she was only there to sleep.

She lay awake until the frantic muffled conclusion of Jake and Yvette's activity, and then listened as their breathing slowed and became regular. She had just drifted off again when there was a whisper in her ear.

". . . and I'm actually pretty sorry about that," Yvette was saying.

"Sure, okay," Leslie said.

"I just think it's important to follow certain paths that present themselves," Yvette said. "That way I have fewer regrets and want to kill myself less often."

Leslie didn't say anything. Yvette seemed to believe that the world had infinite patience with her. Maybe it had so far; maybe it did. Leslie was not the world, though. And it had gotten late.

"I don't think Jake is exceptional, if you were feeling some kind of anxiety about that," Yvette said.

"Thanks," Leslie said.

There was a long silence. It seemed possible that Yvette had fallen asleep. Leslie hoped this was the case.

"Can I tell you that you're beautiful?" Yvette said.

"Please don't," Leslie said.

Yvette reached out and brushed her fingers distractedly through Leslie's damp, tangled hair.

"I get it, you know?" Yvette said. "Like, I *get it*. And I think you do, too. Not many people do."

Leslie shifted closer to her. She wanted to make sure she was understood.

"There's nothing to get, Yvette," she said. "Except, in your case, fucked."

Yvette continued to stroke her hair, unfazed.

"I could get rich," she said. "I could get sick. Hey, pretty soon I'm going to get divorced."

"Jesus," Leslie said.

Yvette exhaled a hard, warm breath into her face.

"I know," she said. "*So* many options."

Acknowledgments

I'm grateful to:

Molly Atlas at ICM;

Jeremy M. Davies, Deborah Ghim, Lauren Roberts, and Rodrigo Corral at FSG;

Laura Kolbe, Sara Martin, and Nick Tenev;

David Gates, Lee Johnson, Amanda Korman, Jordan Rossen, Emma Törzs, and many other friends and colleagues for their advice and editorial interventions;

Lorin Stein and Nicole Rudick at *The Paris Review*, Laura Cogan at *ZYZZYVA*, and Medaya Ocher and Sara Davis at the *Los Angeles Review of Books Quarterly* for editing and publishing earlier versions of some of these stories;

The MacDowell Colony for time to work;

My parents, for everything else.

A Note About the Author

Andrew Martin's first novel, *Early Work*, published by Farrar, Straus and Giroux, was named a *New York Times* Notable Book of 2018. His stories and essays have been published in *The Paris Review*, *The New York Review of Books*, *Harper's Magazine*, and elsewhere. In recent years he has lived in Virginia, Boston, and New York with his partner, Laura, and their dog, Bonnie.